Arthur W. Pinero

The Benefit of the Doubt

A Comedy in Three Acts

Arthur W. Pinero

The Benefit of the Doubt
A Comedy in Three Acts

ISBN/EAN: 9783744783330

Printed in Europe, USA, Canada, Australia, Japan

Cover: Foto ©Andreas Hilbeck / pixelio.de

More available books at **www.hansebooks.com**

THE

BENEFIT OF THE DOUBT

A COMEDY IN THREE ACTS

BY

ARTHUR W. PINERO

RAHWAY, N. J.
THE MERSHON COMPANY
1895

THE MERSHON COMPANY PRESS,
RAHWAY, N. J.

This play was produced at the Comedy Theatre, London, on Wednesday, October 16, 1895.

THE PERSONS OF THE PLAY.

Mrs. Emptage (*a widow*).

Claude Emptage (*her son*).

Justina Emptage
Theophila Fraser } (*her daughters*).

Sir Fletcher Portwood, M. P. (*her brother*).

Mrs. Cloys (*her sister*).

Rt. Rev. Anthony Cloys, D. D., Bishop of St. Olpherts.

Alexander Fraser—"Fraser of Locheen."

John Allingham.

Olive Allingham.

Denzil Shafto
Peter Elphick } (*Allingham's friends*).

Mrs. Quinton Twelves.

Horton (*a servant at Mrs. Emptage's*).

Quaife (*a servant at Mr. Allingham's*).

———

The scenes are placed at Mrs. Emptage's house, in the neighbourhood of Regent's Park, and at The Lichens, Mr. Allingham's cottage at Epsom.

The events of the First and Second Acts occur on the same day; those of the Third Act about fifteen hours afterwards.

THE BENEFIT OF THE DOUBT.

THE FIRST ACT.

The Scene represents a drawing-room in MRS. EMPTAGE'S *house near Regent's Park. At the back are double doors, opening on to a further drawing-room, and these face a window, over which the blinds are drawn, to moderate the glare of the sun, which nevertheless streams through them, for it is a fine afternoon in early summer. The rooms are furnished and decorated in a costly and tasteful fashion.*

MRS. EMPTAGE *is reclining upon the settee, her eyes closed, a bottle of smelling salts in her hand.* JUSTINA *is pacing the room between the door and the window.* MRS. EMPTAGE *is a pretty, carefully preserved woman with dyed hair and "touched-up" face: she is old enough to be the mother of a daughter of nine-and-twenty.* JUSTINA *is of that age, good-looking, "smart," and already somewhat passé. Both are fashionably but sombrely dressed.*

MRS. EMPTAGE.

Tell me the time once more, 'Tina.

JUSTINA.

[*Referring to her watch.*]   A few minutes to four, mother.

MRS. EMPTAGE.

Does the judge of the Divorce Court invariably rise at four o'clock?

JUSTINA.

He may sit a little later under special circumstances.

· MRS. EMPTAGE.

To have done with a case if it's very near its end?

JUSTINA.

So I'm told.

MRS. EMPTAGE.

They must all be here soon, whether that happens or not.

JUSTINA.

Yes, yes. Oh, but if the confounded thing should last into another day!

MRS. EMPTAGE.

A third day's suspense will kill me.

JUSTINA.

Ma, I suppose, really, we ought to be reading our Church Services or something.

MRS. EMPTAGE.

˗ I can't concentrate my attention in the least; I *have* been glancing at "The Yellow Book."

JUSTINA.

Hark! what's that?

MRS. EMPTAGE.

I don't hear anything.

JUSTINA.

It *is* somebody! .

HORTON, *a manservant, appears.*

HORTON.

Mrs. Quinton Twelves.

[MRS. EMPTAGE *struggles to her feet as* MRS.
QUINTON TWELVES *enters.* HORTON
retires. KATE TWELVES *is a lively,
handsome young woman, brightly
dressed.*

JUSTINA AND MRS. EMPTAGE.

[*Throwing themselves upon her.*] Kitty!

MRS. QUINTON TWELVES.

[*Kissing them.*] Well, well, well, well!

JUSTINA.

Is it over?

MRS. QUINTON TWELVES.

Not quite; that is, it wasn't when I came
away. It's all over by now, I expect.

MRS. EMPTAGE.

[*Hysterically.*] Oh, Kitty —— !

Mrs. Quinton Twelves.

S-s-sh, s-s-sh! everything has gone swimmingly, I tell you.

Justina.

For Theophila?

Mrs. Quinton Twelves.

Of course, for Theophila.

Mrs. Emptage.

[*Sinking back on to the settee.*] I felt sure it would.

Justina.

But what was happening when you left?

Mrs. Quinton Twelves.

The dear old judge was just beginning to deliver his decision—his judgment.

Justina.

Oh, how *could* you come away then?

Mrs. Quinton Twelves.

Certainly, it was a wrench. Only, Theo wrote little notes to Sir Fletcher Portwood and to Claude and me. [*Taking a screw of paper from her glove.*] Here's mine. [*Reading.*] " I won't have anybody I am fond of, except my husband, in Court at the finish. They tell me they are sure I am cleared, but it frightens me to think you are all *waiting*. Go to mother's."

MRS. EMPTAGE.

[*Taking the note.*] My poor child! [*Reading it.*] ".... they are sure I am cleared ...." 'Tina, she's cleared!

MRS. QUINTON TWELVES.

Cleared! I wish you could have heard Sir John Clarkson's opening speech for Theophila this morning. There was quite a murmur of approval when he sat down.

JUSTINA.

He let that wretch, Mrs. Jack Allingham, have it—eh? He did!

MRS. QUINTON TWELVES.

He said that a morbidly jealous wife is one of the saddest spectacles the world presents; but that when her jealousy leads her to attempt to blacken the reputation, the hitherto spotless reputation, of another woman,—in this instance, a young lady more happily married than herself,—then that jealous wife becomes a positive danger to society.

MRS. EMPTAGE.

I ought to have been there, 'Tina. I said it was my duty, if you remember.

JUSTINA.

I might have gone.

MRS. QUINTON TWELVES.

Certainly; and yet you have both sat at home, quaking; behaving, for all the world, as if you have a lurking suspicion that Theophila really may—really has—really did——

MRS. EMPTAGE.

Kate, I will not permit you to say such a thing !

MRS. QUINTON TWELVES.

Why these miserable-looking gowns, then ? You are dressed more funereally to-day than you were yesterday !

MRS. EMPTAGE.

[*Tearfully.*] If you live to see a daughter of yours, however innocent she may be, dragged through the Divorce Court——!

JUSTINA.

We haven't been quite certain what we ought to put on.

MRS. EMPTAGE.

I considered half-mourning rather a happy thought.

MRS. QUINTON TWELVES.

To my mind, it looks as if you had deliberately prepared for all emergencies.

MRS. EMPTAGE.

[*Rising, in a flutter.*] 'Tina, pin some flowers in your dress at once ! I'll get Bristow to stick a bit of relief about me somewhere. And I'll wear some more rings——

- [*She goes out.* JUSTINA *selects some cut flowers from a vase on the pianoforte.*

JUSTINA.

Oh, Kit, we were dreadfully in the dumps.
Bless you for bullying us !

MRS. QUINTON TWELVES.

[*Taking a pin from her hat.*] Come here.

JUSTINA.

[*Going to* MRS. TWELVES.] By Jove, though !
it would have been *too* rough on us if—if—
wouldn't it ?

MRS. QUINTON TWELVES.

[*Attaching the flowers to the bodice of* JUSTINA'S
dress.] Pray complete your sentence.

JUSTINA.

Well—if Mrs. Allingham had made out her
case against Jack Allingham and Theo.

MRS. QUINTON TWELVES.

For shame, 'Tina !

JUSTINA.

Oh, you're awfully prudish all of a sudden,
Kate. You've very soon forgotten—— Mind
that pin !

MRS. QUINTON TWELVES.

What are you saying ?

JUSTINA.

I mean, it isn't as if we hadn't all been just a
leetle rapid in our time, we three girls—Theo, you,

and I. You needn't be quite so newly-married-
womanish with *me*.

MRS. QUINTON TWELVES.

Shut up !

JUSTINA.

[*Glancing round.*] No one's there.

MRS. QUINTON TWELVES.

[*In an undertone.*] We always knew where to
draw the line, I hope.

JUSTINA.

Of course we did. Only, when you're married,
as Theo is, to a cold, dry mummy of a man like
Alexander Fraser, the line's apt to get drawn
rather zigzag.

MRS. QUINTON TWELVES.

[*Finishing with the flowers.*] Go away !

JUSTINA.

Thanks—they're jolly. [*Picking up a little
mirror from the table and making a wry face at
herself.*] I haven't had a night's sound sleep for
weeks.

MRS. QUINTON TWELVES.

I should think not, with such thoughts in your
head. Poor Theo ! I've been fretting about her
too, in a different way.

JUSTINA.

[*Adjusting the flowers with the aid of the mirror.*]
Yes, but it isn't only Theo. I've been doing a bit
of lying-awake on my own account, I can tell you.

MRS. QUINTON TWELVES.
Why?

JUSTINA.

[*Moistening her eyelashes as she again surveys
her face.*] Why, if this business had gone against
my sister, it wouldn't have bettered *my* chances
—eh?

MRS. QUINTON TWELVES.
No, perhaps it wouldn't.

JUSTINA.
I'm twenty—oh, you know——

MRS. QUINTON TWELVES.
Nine.

JUSTINA.
Ugh, dash it, yes! And this beastly scrape of
Theophila's has been no end of a shocker for me.
From to-day I turn over the proverbial new leaf.

MRS. QUINTON TWELVES.
So glad, dear.

JUSTINA.
Just fancy! I'm the only single one out of we
three musketeers. Great Scot, Kate, suppose I got
left!

Mrs. Quinton Twelves.

[*With a laugh.*]   'Tina !

Justina.

But I won't, you mark me ! From to-day I'll alter—I take my oath I will ! No more slang for me, no more swears, no more smokes with the men after dinner, no more cycling at the club in knickers ! I've been giving too much away——!

Mrs. Quinton Twelves.

[*Listening.*]   Take care !

Justina.

[*Glancing round.*]   Claude—back.

Claude Emptage, *a plain, stumpy, altogether insignificant young man, enters—a young man with a pale face, red eyelids and nostrils, dense look, and heavy, depressed manner.*

Justina.

What news ?   Any ?

Claude.

It's finished.

Mrs. Quinton Twelves.

Finished !

Justina.

Don't tell me !   How ?

Claude.

It's all right for Theo. Mrs. Allingham's petition dismissed.

JUSTINA.

Ho, ho! Ha, ha, ha! All right for Theo! [*Clapping her hands, almost dancing.* MRS. TWELVES *embraces her.*] All right for Theo!

MRS. QUINTON TWELVES.

Isn't it splendid?

JUSTINA.

Ha, ha, ha! All right for——! Mother! ma! ma! [*She runs out.*

MRS. QUINTON TWELVES.

[*To* CLAUDE.] You did wait, then, in spite of Theo's orders?

CLAUDE.

No, not in Court. I hung about outside, with Uncle Fletcher, to hear the result. [*Sitting, with a little groan.*] Oh!

MRS. QUINTON TWELVES.

I must say, Claude, the victory hasn't left you very cheerful.

CLAUDE.

Cheerful! Think of the day I've spent!

MRS. QUINTON TWELVES.

You've spent!

CLAUDE.

Theophila's brother! [*Pointing into space.*] The brother of Mrs. Fraser of Locheen! The brother of the witness in the box! Every eye upon me!

MRS. QUINTON TWELVES.

[*Drily.*]   I see.

CLAUDE.

Oh, Kate, I've felt this business in more ways than one.   It has been a terrible lesson to me.

MRS. QUINTON TWELVES.

[*Smiling.*]   My poor Claudio !

CLAUDE.

[*Not looking at her.*]   No, don't pity me—despise me.   Kitty, how easy it is for a fellow to imperil a woman's reputation !

MRS. QUINTON TWELVES.

[*Amused.*]   Yes, isn't it ?

CLAUDE.

We attach ourselves to a pretty married woman ; we lounge in her drawing-room, her boudoir ; we make her our toy, our pastime.   Do we allow a single thought of the scandal we may involve her in to check us in our pursuit of pleasure ?

MRS. QUINTON TWELVES.

[*Demurely.*]   No, I suppose you don't.

CLAUDE.

Never !

MRS. QUINTON TWELVES.

Perhaps you had better not come to tea with me quite so frequently in the future, Claude.

CLAUDE.

You are right ; you, and others, must see less of me. [*Turning to her.*] And yet, Kate, I am not all bad !

SIR FLETCHER PORTWOOD *enters. He is fifty-one, amiable, pompous, egotistical, foolish.*

SIR FLETCHER PORTWOOD.

Why didn't you wait for me, Claude, my boy ?

CLAUDE.

Sorry; my brain was reeling.

SIR FLETCHER PORTWOOD.

[*Meeting* MRS. TWELVES.] A very proper, a very satisfactory termination of this affair, Mrs. Twelves.

MRS. QUINTON TWELVES.

It has been awfully reassuring to see you beaming in Court, Sir Fletcher.

SIR FLETCHER PORTWOOD.

Ha ! I daresay my attitude has been remarked. Beaming ; why not ? I've had no doubt as to the result.

MRS. QUINTON TWELVES.

No doubt of Theo's innocence—of course not.

SIR FLETCHER PORTWOOD.

Innocent ; that goes without saying—my niece. But the result, in any case, would have been much the same, I venture to think.

MRS. QUINTON TWELVES.

Really ?

SIR FLETCHER PORTWOOD.

You see, my own public position, if I may speak
of it——

MRS. QUINTON TWELVES.

Oh, yes.

SIR FLETCHER PORTWOOD.

[*Smiling.*] And I happen to know the judge—
slightly, perhaps ; but there it is.

MRS. QUINTON TWELVES.

But judges are not influenced by considerations
of that kind ?

SIR FLETCHER PORTWOOD.

Heaven forbid I should say a word against our
method of administering law in this country.   The
House knows my opinion of the English Judicial
Bench.   At the same time, judges are mortal—I
have never concealed that from myself ; and Sir
William and I have met.   [*To* CLAUDE.] You saw
the judge look at me this morning, Claude ?

CLAUDE.

No.

SIR FLETCHER PORTWOOD.

No ? Oh, yes, and I half-smiled in return.
Yesterday I couldn't catch his eye, but to-day
I've been half-smiling at him all through the pro-
ceedings.

JUSTINA *runs in, seats herself at the pianoforte, and
thumps out the Wedding March.*

JUSTINA.

Well, Uncle Fletcher !

SIR FLETCHER PORTWOOD.

Ah ! ha !

JUSTINA.

What price Mrs. Allingham ?

MRS. EMPTAGE *returns. She has relieved the heaviness of her dress by a fichu of* crêpe de soie.

MRS. EMPTAGE.

[*Embracing* CLAUDE.] My darling ! [*Embracing* SIR FLETCHER.] Oh, my dear Fletcher ! Be quiet, 'Tina !

> [JUSTINA *plays the air of a popular music-hall melody softly ;* MRS. TWELVES *comes to her.*

SIR FLETCHER PORTWOOD.

I told you so—hey !

MRS. EMPTAGE.

We all said so.

SIR FLETCHER PORTWOOD.

But I have been most emphatic——

MRS. EMPTAGE.

Where are Theo and Alec ?

SIR FLETCHER PORTWOOD.

They went over to Sir John Clarkson's chambers directly the case concluded—I fancy, to con-

sult him on some little point that had arisen.   I
managed to get one word——

MRS. EMPTAGE.

[*Impulsively kissing* MRS. TWELVES.]   I'm
so happy !

SIR FLETCHER PORTWOOD.

I contrived to get just one word with Alec as
he was putting Theophila into the carriage.   I
wanted to tell him——

MRS. EMPTAGE.

[*Pacing the room, humming the air played by*
JUSTINA.]   Tra, la, la ! la, la ! tra, la, la !

SIR FLETCHER PORTWOOD.

I wanted to tell him an amusing story I'd heard
during the luncheon interval, but he hadn't time
to—— Ha, ha !   It's a legal anecdote.   It appears that a fellow of the name of Babbitt once
brought an action——

MRS. EMPTAGE.

Did the judge apologise, Fletcher ?

[JUSTINA *stops playing.*

SIR FLETCHER PORTWOOD.

Apologise !

MRS. EMPTAGE.

To Theophila ?

SIR FLETCHER PORTWOOD.

A judge never apologises.

MRS. EMPTAGE.

He might do worse, where such undeserved distress is occasioned a young wife and her husband——

MRS. QUINTON TWELVES.

Hear, hear !

MRS. EMPTAGE.

To say nothing of her mother !

SIR FLETCHER PORTWOOD.

I surmise that the judgment of my friend Sir William was very strongly worded, and I daresay an expression of regret followed from Mrs. Allingham's counsel. But I had quitted the Court, you know——

MRS. EMPTAGE.

Oh, yes ; Theo wrote you a note——

SIR FLETCHER PORTWOOD.

But you are losing my anecdote. It appears that a man of the name of Babbitt—— One thing, Muriel, I will stake my reputation upon.

MRS. EMPTAGE.

[*Peeping out at the side of the window blind.*] What's that ?

SIR FLETCHER PORTWOOD.

That the public applauded the decision roundly.

MRS. EMPTAGE.

[*Pacing the room again.*] I can hear them doing it ! Bravo, Mrs. Fraser ! Eh, girls ?

Mrs. Quinton Twelves.

Plucky Mrs. Fraser !

Justina.

How jolly to have been there just then !

Sir Fletcher Portwood.

As a matter of fact, I talked with several strangers of a humble rank of life, and hinted that a few cheers—so regrettable and unseemly in a court of law as a rule—I hinted that a few cheers would undoubtedly be justifiable in the present instance, as well as peculiarly agreeable to me. It seems that Babbitt——

Horton *enters with a card.*

Mrs. Emptage.

[*After glancing at the card.*] Oh——

Sir Fletcher Portwood.

Eh !

Justina.

What's up ?

Mrs. Emptage.

[*To* Horton.] Where *is* Mrs. Cloys ?

[Sir Fletcher, Justina, *and* Claude *rise precipitately.*

Horton.

In the morning-room, ma'am. She preferred——

MRS. EMPTAGE.

[*Taking the card.*]   I—I—someone will come to
her.   [HORTON *retires.*

SIR FLETCHER PORTWOOD.

Harriet here !

JUSTINA.

By Jove !

CLAUDE.

[*Making for the door.*]   No ; she is too impossible.

MRS. EMPTAGE.

[*Intercepting him.*]   Claude, I dare you to leave
the house !

[SIR FLETCHER *also moves towards the door.*

MRS. EMPTAGE.

[*Stopping him.*]   Fletcher, you mustn't !

SIR FLETCHER PORTWOOD.

Muriel, I distinctly prefer not to meet——

MRS. EMPTAGE.

But I must have every support ; I am unequal
to it otherwise. Who will fetch her upstairs?
Fletcher, dear !——

SIR FLETCHER PORTWOOD.

In your establishment ! Singularly inappro-
priate !

MRS. EMPTAGE.

[*Turning to* JUSTINA.]   Justina——

JUSTINA.

No, thanks, ma.

MRS. EMPTAGE.

Brutes, all of you !   [*She hurries out.*

JUSTINA.

Confound her !

CLAUDE.

I shall submit to none of her airs. What *is* a bishop ?

SIR FLETCHER PORTWOOD.

Why does she select this occasion——

JUSTINA.

It's nearly ten years since she washed her hands of us.

SIR FLETCHER PORTWOOD.

Exactly eleven years have elapsed since my sister Harriet placed it out of my power to continue on a footing of brotherly intercourse with her.

CLAUDE.

[*To* MRS. TWELVES, *in a whisper.*]   I know the story.

JUSTINA.

[*To him.*]   S-s-sh !

SIR FLETCHER PORTWOOD.

Her behaviour on that one memorable afternoon proved that her marriage to a dignitary of the Church was something worse than a fluke—a sacrilege.

Mrs. Quinton Twelves.
[*Quietly to* Claude.] What is it?

Claude.
[*Quietly to her.*] She called him a Bore.

Mrs. Quinton Twelves.
[*Going to* Justina.] Do you think I could steal downstairs and get away? She used to tell me I was an empty-headed little fool.

Sir Fletcher Portwood.
Outrageous!

Mrs. Quinton Twelves.
And predicted I should end badly.

Justina.
Well, you haven't.

Mrs. Quinton Twelves.
No, but there's time, she'd say. [*Going towards the door.*] I'm off.

Justina.
Sneak!

Mrs. Quinton Twelves.
[*Returning hastily.*] They're coming up!

Justina.
Let 'em!

Mrs. Cloys *enters, and stands surveying the room.* Mrs. Emptage *follows her.* Mrs. Cloys *is about fifty-three, handsome, dignified in bearing, richly but soberly dressed, in manner a mixture of sweetness and acerbity.*

MRS. CLOYS.

Justina—is it ?

JUSTINA.

[*Going to her.*]   How do you do, Aunt Harriet ?

MRS. CLOYS.

[*Kissing her, then eyeing her keenly.*]   H'm ! *you're* not married yet, I believe ?

JUSTINA.

No, I haven't the slightest inclination that way.

MRS. CLOYS.

Oh, my dear, you still tell fibs, then !

JUSTINA.

Indeed, aunt ?

[JUSTINA *retires ;* SIR FLETCHER *advances.* MRS. CLOYS *kisses him, then looks him up and down.*

MRS. CLOYS.

Well, Fletcher, so they've knighted you, have they?

SIR FLETCHER PORTWOOD.

Lord Cranbery was gracious enough to recommend——

MRS. CLOYS.

How much did it cost you?

SIR FLETCHER PORTWOOD.

Cost me!

MRS. CLOYS.

Well, you've made money; I suppose you could afford it.

SIR FLETCHER PORTWOOD.

Pray let us——

MRS. CLOYS.

Don't puff yourself out at me, Fletcher.

SIR FLETCHER PORTWOOD.

I am doing nothing of the kind, Harriet.

MRS. CLOYS.

Then don't.

SIR FLETCHER PORTWOOD.

Er—how is the bishop?

MRS. CLOYS.

Old.

SIR FLETCHER PORTWOOD.

Old? Let me see—my marvellous head for figures should serve me——

MRS. CLOYS.

Very old.

SIR FLETCHER PORTWOOD.

Born in——

MRS. CLOYS.

We're all getting old ; that's why you have the pleasure of seeing me amongst you once more. [*Turning to* CLAUDE, *who bows stiffly.*] My nephew? [*Shaking hands with him and looking him in the face searchingly.*] You're rather old too. [*Sharply.*] Who's that there?

MRS. QUINTON TWELVES.

[*Who has been hidden by the flowers on the piano-forte, advancing with a nervous outburst.*] Oh, I hope you remember me, dear Mrs. Cloys— Kitty Twelves. I was Kitty Powis, if you recollect.

MRS. CLOYS.

I recollect. Weren't you at school in Paris with Justina and Theophila, and afterwards——

MRS. QUINTON TWELVES.

Yes. Isn't this interesting? Quinton, my husband, was *confirmed* by the Bishop of St. Olpherts! I never discovered it till we'd been married for ages—I mean, weeks and weeks—[*gradually quailing under* MRS. CLOY's *gaze*]—and then one day— he—he happened to see me kissing the sweetest photograph of you—and—and—and——

MRS. CLOYS.

Mrs. Twills, I understood from my sister there was a purely family gathering here this afternoon——

Mrs. Quinton Twelves.

[*Offering her hand.*] I—I have to go on elsewhere——

Mrs. Cloys.

[*Detaining her hand.*] My dear, *you* were extremely old when I last saw you, during your first
season, in eighty something; I pray, now you're
married, that you are—younger.

> [*They look at each other for a moment
> longer, then* Mrs. Twelves *withdraws
> her hand, and, after nodding to the
> others in a scared way, goes out silently.*
> Claude *follows her.*

Mrs. Cloys.

[*Sitting on the settee.*] Muriel. [Mrs. Emptage *comes to her.*] We have been on bad terms
for many years ; let us have done with it. I suggest mutual concessions to disposition and temper.

Mrs. Emptage.

[*Sitting.*] I am sure I have been more than
desirous——

Mrs. Cloys.

You have brought up your children abominably ;
that was always our most serious point of dissen-
sion——

Sir Fletcher Portwood.

I may remind you, Harriet, that Muriel's cheerful method of training her children has received
my sympathy and sanction. On the death of the
late Mr. Emptage——

MRS. EMPTAGE.

My poor dear Herbert——

SIR FLETCHER PORTWOOD.

It naturally devolved upon me——

MRS. CLOYS.

S-s-sh !

SIR FLETCHER PORTWOOD.

I am not one of those——

MRS. CLOYS.

S-s-sh, s-s-sh, s-s-sh !

MRS. EMPTAGE.

Your twenty years of married life may have taught you how to manage a husband, Harriet, but——

SIR FLETCHER PORTWOOD.

Heaven has blessed you with no offspring.

MRS. EMPTAGE.

And the world isn't all deans, and canons, and bishops and things——

SIR FLETCHER PORTWOOD.

A department of society you were thrown head-long into——

MRS. EMPTAGE.

By the merest chance, as you well know——

Sir Fletcher Portwood.

Without, I fear, possessing every qualification for the—ah—the exalted station which— which——

Mrs. Emptage.

And—and—and——

Mrs. Cloys.

[*To* Mrs. Emptage.] There, there! Don't I say, Have done with it? At any rate, we're gray-haired women now—I *am*, and you ought to be——

Mrs. Emptage.

Now, Harriet——

Mrs. Cloys.

And judgment has overtaken you——

Mrs. Emptage.

Judgment !

Mrs. Cloys.

This terrible calamity that has befallen your girl Theophila. Oh, how is it going to end !

Mrs. Emptage.

My dear Harriet, it has ended.

Mrs. Cloys.

Has the case——

Sir Fletcher Portwood.

Mrs. Allingham's petition is dismissed — dismissed.

MRS. EMPTAGE.

My daughter has emerged triumphantly——

MRS. CLOYS.

Thank God ! [*Rising.*] Muriel——
　[MRS. EMPTAGE *rises ;* MRS. CLOYS *kisses
　her on both cheeks, then turns away.*

MRS. EMPTAGE.

You will see Theo and her husband in a few
minutes. They are staying with me just now.
"Weak, giddy mother," am I, Harriet? My
child flies to me in her trouble, nevertheless.

MRS. CLOYS.

[*Wiping her eyes.*] The dear bishop will be so
rejoiced. Not a newspaper has been taken at the
Palace this week. [*Resuming her seat.*] It has
hit us hard. How did it all come about?

SIR FLETCHER PORTWOOD.

In this way. I——

MRS. EMPTAGE.

[*Sitting again.*] Why, we've all known Jack
Allingham for years——

SIR FLETCHER PORTWOOD.

[*Sitting.*] A good fellow—little dull, perhaps—
little prosy——

MRS. EMPTAGE.

[*Glancing at* JUSTINA.] At one time we
thought he was rather inclined to pay 'Tina——

JUSTINA.

What rot, mother !

MRS. CLOYS.

Oh !

MRS. EMPTAGE.

However, he married this creature, Olive Harker—daughter of a Major Harker——

SIR FLETCHER PORTWOOD.

"Crummy" Harker—stout man——

JUSTINA.

Four years ago this month.

MRS. EMPTAGE.

Yes, in the summer of the year in which Theo was married to Fraser of Locheen.

SIR FLETCHER PORTWOOD.

My extraordinary chronological faculty ought to serve me here. Theophila and Locheen were married in the March, Jack Allingham and Miss Harker in the following June ; *I* took the chair that year at no less than three public dinners——

MRS. EMPTAGE.

Of course, when the two couples settled down in London the usual exchange of visits began. But from the first it was quite evident that Mrs. Allingham resented her husband's friendship for Theo.

MRS. CLOYS.

Why should Mrs. Allingham have resented it?

JUSTINA.

Olive was always a jealous cat—person.

SIR FLETCHER PORTWOOD.

John is some months younger than his wife, I
may tell you. No marriage can turn out happily
when the balance of age drops ever so slightly on
the woman's side. My observation——

MRS. CLOYS.

Rubbish !

SIR FLETCHER PORTWOOD.

I know my world, Harriet.

JUSTINA.

What was it that Olive said about that, ma?

MRS. EMPTAGE.

When the wife is older than the husband every
fresh little line in her face becomes an acute pain
to her, just as if it were cut into her flesh, and
renewed daily, with a knife. Those are Mrs.
Allingham's own words.

MRS. CLOYS.

Poor wretch !

MRS. EMPTAGE.

In her storms with Jack she used to rave out
these things, and Jack would repeat them to Theo.

MRS. CLOYS.

What business had he to do that, pray?

MRS. EMPTAGE.

Well, his home had become such a hell that he fell into the way of rushing round to Lennox Gardens, to Theophila and Alec, to obtain relief from his worries.

JUSTINA.

He gradually became a sort of third in Lennox Gardens, you know, aunt.

MRS. CLOYS.

A sort of third?

MRS. EMPTAGE.

The house-friend who is continually running in and out——

JUSTINA.

The man who has dined with you almost before you know it, as it were.

MRS. CLOYS.

Oh! And is this all?

MRS. EMPTAGE.

All?

MRS. CLOYS.

All the justification a jealous woman has for seeking to divorce her husband?

SIR FLETCHER PORTWOOD.

Not divorce, Harriet ; she wasn't entitled to
ask for that. Mrs. Allingham has been suing for
judicial separation.

MRS. CLOYS.

Well, well——

SIR FLETCHER PORTWOOD.

Accuracy with me is a perfect mania. Oh, yes,
that's all. With the exception of the—the——
[*With a wave of the hand.*] However——

MRS. CLOYS.

Exception ?

SIR FLETCHER PORTWOOD.

I was thinking of the bézique part of the case.

MRS. EMPTAGE.

[*Impatiently.*] Yes, yes : but that's of no consequence now.

MRS. CLOYS.

Bézique?

SIR FLETCHER PORTWOOD.

Allingham and Theophila happen, both of them,
to be fond of cards. And when Fraser was away
in Scotland——

MRS. CLOYS.

Away in Scotland ? *Not* with Theophila ?

SIR FLETCHER PORTWOOD.

No, no ; she loathes Locheen.

MRS. CLOYS.

I see. When Mr. Fraser was in Scotland and his wife was by herself in London——

MRS. EMPTAGE.

Then a little harmless bézique helped to kill the time.

MRS. CLOYS.

Theophila and Mr. Allingham killed time together?

MRS. EMPTAGE, JUSTINA, SIR FLETCHER.

[*In various tones.*] Yes—yes—yes.

MRS. CLOYS.

Where was the time killed?

SIR FLETCHER PORTWOOD.

In Lennox Gardens.

MRS. CLOYS.

At Theophila's house, in her husband's absence. Is *that* all?

MRS. EMPTAGE.

Absolutely all.

SIR FLETCHER PORTWOOD.

All the bézique part of the case. You see, the lawyers separated the case against Theophila into three divisions.

MRS. CLOYS.

Three! Number one?

Sir Fletcher Portwood.
The House-friend, as aforesaid.

Mrs. Cloys.
Two ?

Sir Fletcher Portwood.
Bézique—as aforesaid.

Mrs. Cloys.
Three ?

Mrs. Emptage.
I repeat, surely all this doesn't matter now.

Mrs. Cloys.
Number three ?

Sir Fletcher Portwood.
Tannhäuser.

Mrs. Cloys.
In Heaven's name, what——

Justina.
That was nothing.   Alec Fraser was in Scotland as usual——

Mrs. Cloys.
As usual !

Mrs. Emptage.
No, no—as he is often obliged to be.

Justina.
-Alec was in Scotland, and Theo had been to the opera with pals——

MRS. CLOYS.
With——

JUSTINA.
Friends, to hear Tannhäuser. She had sent her servants to bed, and let herself in with her latch-key. As she was closing the front door she caught sight of Jack Allingham on the other side of the way.

MRS. EMPTAGE.
He had had one of his terrible scenes with his wife; they lived round the corner, in Pont Street——

SIR FLETCHER PORTWOOD.
And a most charming house theirs was. I always say, with regard to Pont Street——

MRS. CLOYS.
[*Sternly.*] Fletcher!

MRS. EMPTAGE.
Jack was in a dreadful state of distress; pacing the streets like a maniac, in fact——

JUSTINA.
He's a very old friend of all of us——

MRS. EMPTAGE.
More like a brother than a——

JUSTINA.
And Theo begged him to come in——

Mrs. Emptage.

To calm himself. Simply an impulsive, warm-hearted act on her part.

Justina.

And it wouldn't have mattered in the least if that devil of a wife hadn't suspected——

Mrs. Emptage.

And planted her maid outside Theo's house—set of spies !——

Sir Fletcher Portwood.

Till three in the morning——

Mrs. Emptage.

When Theo turned Jack out.

Sir Fletcher Portwood.

Not *four* in the morning, as Mrs. Allingham's blundering counsel tried to establish. Ha, ha ! Sir John Clarkson bowled him over there ! Three sir, not four !

Mrs. Cloys.

[*To* Sir Fletcher.] Be quiet ! be silent !

Sir Fletcher Portwood.

Upon my word, Harriet——

Mrs. Cloys.

[*To* Justina, *who rises.*] Go away ! You can sit by and assist at the telling of a story of this nature, single woman that you are ! [Justina *walks away.*] What did I prophesy? Years ago, what did I prophesy? [*To* Mrs. Emptage.] Now, pray, how do you like seeing your children dabbling their hands in this—this pig-pail?

Claude *enters.*

Claude.

Fraser and Theo——

Mrs. Emptage.

[*Rising.*] Ah!

Claude.

Just come in.

[Mrs. Cloys *walks away ;* Claude *joins* Justina.

Mrs. Emptage.

[*Repressing her excitement.*] S-s-sh, s-s sh, s-s-sh! Let nobody make a fuss ; Alec hates a fuss.

Sir Fletcher Portwood.

No fuss, but someone ought to play "See the Conquering Hero——!" Theo is so fond of a little fun—genuine fun!

[*He seats himself at the piano and fingers out the air laboriously.* Theophila *and her husband enter. She is an elegantly dressed, still girlish, woman of seven-and-twenty ; he a good-looking, unde-monstrative man of about five-and-thirty. Both are pale, weary-looking, and subdued.* Fraser *is gloved and frock coated ;* Theophila *is in her bonnet and cape.*

MRS. EMPTAGE.

[*Her hand twitching.*] Well, pet?

THEOPHILA.

[*Kissing her mother in a spiritless way.*] Well,
mother dear?

> [THEOPHILA *goes to* JUSTINA *and* CLAUDE
> *and kisses them silently.*

MRS. EMPTAGE.

[*Shaking hands with* FRASER.] A hundred
thousand congratulations, Alec.

FRASER.

[*Biting his lip.*] Thanks. [*Standing at the
further end of the piano, to* SIR FLETCHER.] Do
you mind *not* playing?

SIR FLETCHER PORTWOOD.

[*Rising and singing.*] "See the Conquering
He—ro co—o—o—o—o—o—um—ms!" Not
hero—heroes. No, hero and heroine!

> [THEOPHILA *comes to him and kisses him in
> the same impassive fashion.*

THEOPHILA.

[*Quietly.*] Much obliged to you for sticking
to me, the last two days, uncle.

SIR FLETCHER PORTWOOD.

My dear, as a matter of fact, I've enjoyed myself in Court. I am not exaggerating—enjoyed
myself.

MRS. EMPTAGE.

Theo, your Aunt Harriet——

THEOPHILA.

[*Turning.*]   Aunt——!   [*Advancing slowly to meet* MRS. CLOYS—*a little dazed.*]   I saw a figure ; I—I thought it was Kitty.   Why, aunt——!

[*They shake hands.*

MRS. CLOYS.

[*Looking into her face earnestly.*]   You're tired —quite done.

THEOPHILA.

[*With a nod, sitting on the settee.*]   Alec ! [FRASER *advances.*]   My Aunt Harriet, Mrs. Cloys—my husband.

[FRASER *and* MRS. CLOYS *incline their heads to each other.* FRASER *then turns away and joins* CLAUDE *and* JUSTINA, SIR FLETCHER PORTWOOD *following him.* THEOPHILA *strips off her gloves.*

MRS. EMPTAGE.

Let mother take your bonnet, pet.

THEOPHILA.

[*Her head falling backward, faintly.*]   Oh, do !

MRS. EMPTAGE.

[*Removing* THEOPHILA'S *bonnet.*]   In your bonnet all day again ; your head must be splitting!

I know. Do you remember *my* head at the flower show at Eastbourne?

> [MRS. CLOYS *bends over* THEOPHILA *and helps her to get rid of her cape.*

THEOPHILA.

Thanks, awfully.

> [*She takes her bonnet from* MRS. EMPTAGE, *and fiercely begins to roll it in her cape, as if about to crush them together.*

MRS. EMPTAGE.

[*Uttering a little scream, running round the settee to her.*] What are you doing?

> · [*There is a general movement.*

THEOPHILA.

[*Looking round.*] It's all right. [*With an attempt at a laugh.*] Those things are to be destroyed.

MRS. EMPTAGE.

[*Taking the bonnet and cape from* THEOPHILA.] Destroyed! They were new for the case!

THEOPHILA.

Sniff them, mother.

MRS. EMPTAGE.

[*Doing so.*] Perfume.

THEOPHILA.

Phew! I intend to burn every thread I'm wearing, and to have a bath before dinner.

FRASER.

[*Constrainedly.*] We were rather unfortunate in the case that is to follow ours.

THEOPHILA.

Yes. [*Looking straight before her.*] There was a patchouli business waiting to come on after us.

MRS. EMPTAGE.

[*Holding the things at arm's length.*] Oh, dear !

THEOPHILA.

It had been flitting about since the morning. It sat down beside me at last.

MRS. EMPTAGE.

It ?

THEOPHILA.

It, it, it ! And it was wearing a bonnet almost precisely like mine ; and it looked to be about my own age, and could have had my sort of complexion if it had chosen——

MRS. CLOYS.

Hush, Theophila——!

THEOPHILA.

[*Hysterically.*] Ho, ho, ho! these last two days !

HORTON *enters with tea.*

MRS. EMPTAGE.

Here's tea! Claude, help Justina with the tea-table. Tea is what Theo needs.

> [*She hurries out with* THEOPHILA's *bonnet and cape.* CLAUDE *and* JUSTINA *carry the tea-table and place it before the "cosy corner."* MRS. CLOYS *sits with her head bent.* HORTON *places the tray upon the tea-table and withdraws.* JUSTINA *sits in the "cosy-corner" and pours out tea.*

SIR FLETCHER PORTWOOD.

[*Bustling up to the tea-table.*] Tea is what we *all* need. A most exciting day! I've often observed how welcome one's tea is on a Derby Day——

THEOPHILA.

[*In a whisper to* FRASER *across the table.*] Alec, will you tell them what the judge said of me, or shall I?

FRASER.

I suppose it's necessary.

THEOPHILA.

People *heard* it. Then the papers——

FRASER.

Of course. [*Agitated.*] I—I'll tell them, if you like.

THEOPHILA.

Thank you. [*Quickly.*] No, no—I'll tell them. You couldn't do it—how *could* you ?

[MRS. EMPTAGE *returns.*

MRS. EMPTAGE.

Tea, tea ! [*Sitting.*] Alec, come and sit by me.

[FRASER *sits at a distance, his lips compressed, his hands gripped together.*

MRS. EMPTAGE.

Oh, fie ! all that way off ! You will persist in treating me as an ordinary mother-in-law ! [FRASER *moves his chair a little nearer.*] That's better. [*Triumphantly.*] Well, Harriet, you see all my children round me—a happy family !

[CLAUDE *brings tea to* MRS. CLOYS.

SIR FLETCHER PORTWOOD.

[*Bringing a cup of tea to* THEOPHILA.] I make no excuse for devoting myself to Theo—on this occasion. [THEOPHILA *takes the tea and gulps it.*] You looked charming in the witness-box—piquant. [*Returning to the tea-table.*] Piquant—just the word—piquant.

MRS. EMPTAGE.

Now, Alec dear, tell us. Did Mrs. Allingham's counsel, Mr. What's-his-name, express regret when it was all over ?

FRASER.

Regret——?

[SIR FLETCHER *brings tea to* MRS. EMP-
TAGE ; CLAUDE *brings tea to* FRASER,
then returns to the tea-table.

MRS. EMPTAGE.

Regret at finding himself made the—the thing-
amy—the vehicle—for such a malicious attack on
Theo's character—the poor child.

FRASER.

[*With an effort.*]   No ; no regret was ex-
pressed.

MRS. EMPTAGE.

Not by the judge either ?

FRASER.

The judge !

MRS. EMPTAGE.

The judge never said he was sorry to see a
nicely-bred girl, so recently married too, subjected
to such a—such a—such an unwarrantable ordeal ?
[FRASER *is silent.*]   Eh—h ?

THEOPHILA.

[*After a brief pause.*]   No, mother.

MRS. EMPTAGE.

You were wrong, then, Fletcher, you see.

SIR FLETCHER PORTWOOD.

[*Holding up his hand.*]   Wait, wait, please !
I don't think I am *very* often out in my calcula-

tions. [*To* THEOPHILA.] What sort of demonstration occurred at the close, may I venture to ask?

THEOPHILA.

Demonstration?

MRS. EMPTAGE.

Did they cheer you much, darling? That's what your uncle means.

THEOPHILA.

Cheer me, mother——?
[FRASER *rises abruptly, placing his cup, with a clatter, on the piano.*

FRASER.

I—I feel as Theophila does. I must dip my face into cold water. The atmosphere of that place stifles one even now. Do excuse me.
[*He goes out; all, except* THEOPHILA, *look after him, surprised.*

THEOPHILA.

Mother dear—Uncle Fletcher—you seem to have a wrong impression——

MRS. EMPTAGE.

Wrong impression?

THEOPHILA.

Oh, Mrs. Allingham's petition has been dismissed—yes. But Sir John Clarkson and Mr. Martyn, my other counsel,—all my friends, in fact, —were a little too sanguine.

MRS. EMPTAGE.

Too sanguine?

THEOPHILA.

Oh, much too sanguine. The judge was rather rough on me.

MRS. EMPTAGE.

What on earth do you——?

THEOPHILA.

Rather down on me—severe. My behaviour—my conduct—has been careless—indiscreet, he says——

MRS. EMPTAGE.

[*Under her breath.*] Indiscreet?

THEOPHILA.

Hardly characteristic of a woman who is properly watchful of her own and her husband's reputation—honour.

JUSTINA.

[*Coming forward a few steps.*] Theo!

THEOPHILA.

[*Disjointedly.*] But at the same time, he said, Mrs. Allingham had scarcely succeeded in establishing conclusively to his mind . . . oh ! . . . and he thought that even the petitioner herself, on further reflection, would be desirous that I should receive the—the benefit of the doubt . . . and—and something about costs . . .

[*She breaks off; they all remain silent for a time.*

Mrs. Emptage.

This—this will appear in the papers! Won't it? Won't it? [*No one replies;* Sir Fletcher *sinks into a chair, with a blank look.*] Can't anybody answer me? Fletcher, will this be in the papers?

Sir Fletcher Portwood.

[*Confused.*] The papers——! No strong-minded public man ever looks at the papers. When I have spoken in the House I never——

Justina.

[*In a hard voice.*] Why, of course, a dozen papers will have it. What a silly question to ask, ma!

Mrs. Emptage.

[*Advancing to* Mrs. Cloys.] I hope you're quite satisfied, Harriet. You came here, after these many years, on purpose to witness this— [Mrs. Cloys *rises.*]—to see disgrace and ruin brought on me and my family.

Mrs. Cloys.

Muriel, how dare you say it!

Mrs. Emptage.

I'm only a widow! Everybody is entitled to stab at me!

Mrs. Cloys.

[*Turning away.*] I'll not listen to you!

MRS. EMPTAGE.

[*Weeping.*] Oh, oh, oh ! how glad our friends will be ! [*Going towards the door.*] Here's a triumph for our friends !

JUSTINA.

[*Following her.*] Mother——

MRS. EMPTAGE.

[*Pushing her aside.*] Go away ! I don't want you near me !

JUSTINA.

Ho !

MRS. EMPTAGE.

Bristow shall attend on me. I shall lie down on my bed. I shall have my corsets taken off——
[*She disappears.*

MRS. CLOYS.

[*Going towards the door.*] Muriel——!
[*She goes out, following* MRS. EMPTAGE.

JUSTINA.

[*With a grating laugh.*] That's ma all over ; she always goes through this process when there's a family crisis. [*To* THEOPHILA.] Do you remember, Phil ?

THEOPHILA.

[*Stonily.*] What ?

JUSTINA.

Directly the news of poor pa's death came, ma took off her corsets.

SIR FLETCHER PORTWOOD.

[*Rising.*] I shall go out ; people shall see me walking boldly through the streets : Portland Place—Regent Street—[*in agitation*]—Fletcher Portwood, with his head up—his head up, they'll say. [*He paces the room, and comes upon* CLAUDE, *who is sitting at the writing table, writing a telegram, his eyes bolting and a generally vacuous expression on his face.*] And you ! when are you going to do something in the world besides idling, and loafing, and living upon your mother——?

CLAUDE.

[*Rising, disconcerted.*] What's that to do with it ?

SIR FLETCHER PORTWOOD.

Do with it ? Why, at eighteen I was earning twenty shillings a week, and maintaining myself. Now look at the position I have achieved, from sheer brain-force ! [*To* THEOPHILA.] I shall not turn my back on you, my poor little girl ; don't be frightened of that. You were always my favourite niece——

JUSTINA.

[*Laughing, a little wildly.*] Ha, ha, ha, ha !

SIR FLETCHER PORTWOOD.

I beg your pardon, 'Tina ; I've no favourites. Can I buy you anything, either of you, while I'm out ? I may look in here again before I go down to the House. The finest assembly of gentlemen in the world. No patterns, or new music, wanted —eh ?

Theophila.

[*Feebly.*] Oh, no.

Sir Fletcher Portwood.

I shall dine at the House, and then sup at the club. All London shall see me. " Look at Portwood ! " everybody will say. " Then there can't be the slightest foundation for this scandal about his niece—— ! "   [*He goes out.*

Claude.

[*Looking after him.*] Transparent old egotist ! How do I know whether I'm in his will or not ? And yet I stand here and allow him to lecture me ! Me ! Ha, compare his education with mine ! And what real knowledge has he of Life, of Men and Women—— ? [*Showing* Justina *his telegram.*] Is that the way you spell Bernhart ?

Justina.

[*Reading the telegram.*] No ; h-a-r-*d*-t. What's this ?

Claude.

[*In an undertone.*] The Wartons wanted to take me to see Bernhardt to-night. Of course, I can't go *now*. A marked man ! every eye upon me ! her brother ! [*Going to the door, he meets* Fraser.] 'Ullo, Fraser !

> [Claude *goes out* ; Fraser, *who is carrying his hat and gloves, walks across the room, eyeing* Justina.

Justina.

[*To* Fraser.] Do you want to speak to Theo ?

FRASER.

Oh—just for one moment——

[THEOPHILA *rises ;* JUSTINA *goes to her.*

JUSTINA.

Never mind, old girl. [*With a little laugh.*]
Ha ! I suppose this has queered my pitch for a
season or two, but—[*kissing her*]—never mind—
[*going to the door*]—these things will happen in
the best regulated——

[*She disappears. There is a brief silence,
during which* THEOPHILA *closes the
doors.*

FRASER.

Have you told your people ?

THEOPHILA.

Yes.

FRASER.

How do they take it?

THEOPHILA.

All right—pretty well. Mother is lying down
for a bit. She'll be quite herself again in a few
days.

FRASER.

[*Thoughtfully.*] A few days—will she ?
[*Partly to himself.*] In a few days ?

THEOPHILA.

She'll have a week at Worthing. She's always
had a week at Worthing when we've been in any

trouble. You've got your hat, Alec ; do you mean to dine out?

FRASER.

To-night !

THEOPHILA.

[*Weakly.*] Oh, don't be so sharp with me ! All the way home from the Strand you'd hardly speak a word.

FRASER.

[*Sitting on the settee.*] I was thinking over what we'd been listening to.

THEOPHILA.

Yes, the things sounded much worse in Court than they did out of it, didn't they ?

FRASER.

[*His head bowed.*] Awful !

THEOPHILA.

How cruel it was of them to buoy us up by telling us the case was going right for me !

FRASER.

Many believed it. Martyn was sure the judge was on our side.

THEOPHILA.

When one comes to think of it, her counsel managed to put such a very queer complexion——

FRASER.

Awful.

THEOPHILA.

Oh, I don't know what I felt like at some moments! I—I felt like a woman caught with bare shoulders in daylight.

FRASER.

Awful.

THEOPHILA.

[*Looking at him curiously.*] Alec, you seem to be—different to me, now the trial's over.

FRASER.

[*In a muffled voice.*] Do I? I—we're worn out.

THEOPHILA.

[*After some hesitation, going to the back of the settee.*] I say! I want to tell you—I am—truly sorry.

FRASER.

[*Raising his head.*] Sorry——!

THEOPHILA.

[*With an effort.*] And I humbly beg your pardon.

FRASER.

[*Rising and facing her.*] For what?

THEOPHILA.

Why, for all the bother I've caused.

FRASER.

[*Resuming his seat.*] Oh—— !
    [*She stares at him for a moment, surprised
        and disappointed, then turns away.*

THEOPHILA.

[*To herself.*] Oh——! [*To him.*] Alec, I've
had the idea that the trouble we've lately gone
through, both of us, over this horrid business,
might help to bring us together. We haven't
got along over-well, have we?

FRASER.

Not too well, I'm afraid.

THEOPHILA.

A good deal my fault, I daresay. Oh, I hated
Locheen——!

FRASER.

Yes.

THEOPHILA.

As heartily as you hate London. I'm a town
girl, a thorough little cockney—you knew it when
you married me!—and—Locheen——

FRASER.

Locheen is a beautiful place.

THEOPHILA.

London's a beautiful place.

FRASER.

No.

THEOPHILA.

[*Hotly.*] No to you, then. [*Sitting.*] I beg
pardon again; I didn't mean to be rude. I understand how you feel. You were born at Locheen.

FRASER.

I was.

THEOPHILA.

[*Pointing towards the window.*] I was born in Chester Terrace. I admit, Locheen is all very well at a certain time of year. But to be stuck there when London's full; when nobody but a poor relation, whose. railway ticket you send with the invitation, will come and look you up! Oh, that summer you made me spend there just after we were married!

FRASER.

I was very happy that summer.

THEOPHILA.

You were in love. And then, the pipers! those pipers!

FRASER.

Duncan and Hamish were supremely ridiculous to you, I remember.

THEOPHILA.

Not ridiculous, as you say it—great fun for a time; but four or five months of Duncan and Hamish and their pipes! To and fro on the terrace, for a whole hour in the morning, those pipes! To and fro, up and down, all round the house, in the afternoon, those pipes. At dinner, from the trout to the banana, those pipes. And then, the notion of your persistently dining in a kilt! A Highland costume on the moors—yes; but in the lamplight—at dinner——!

FRASER.

It is my dress ; I don't vary it.

THEOPHILA.

Think of it !   A man and woman dining *tête-à-tête*, for months and months ; the woman hypped, weary ; the novelty of her new clothes gradually wearing off ; she feeling she was getting lean and plain with it all, salt-cellary about the shoulders, drawn and hideous—[*staring before her, her eyes dilating*]—and, every blessed night, the man in a magnificent evening kilt !

FRASER.

Surely that, too, was "great fun" for a time ?

THEOPHILA.

It might have been, if you had the smallest sense of humour, Alec ; but one soon tires of laughing alone.   No, there was never any fun in that kilt.   It got on my nerves from the beginning—the solemn, stupid stateliness of it.   Girls are subject to creeps and crawls ; I grew at last to positively dread joining you in the hall of an evening, to be frightened at giving you my arm to go in to dinner—the simple sound of the rustling of my skirt against that petticoat of yours made the chairs, everything, dance.   At those moments old Duncan and his boy Hamish seemed to be blowing into the blood-vessels of my head.   And during dinner even the table wouldn't help me ; I was weak, hysterical—I declare to goodness I could always see through the thickness of the board—see the two knees! [*With a back-ward shake of the head.*] Ha !

FRASER.

Well, Duncan and Hamish—poor fellows—and their pipes, and the objectionable kilt—those things need never trouble you again ; at any rate, we can decide that.

THEOPHILA.

Oh, no, Alec, we will go up to Locheen in August——

FRASER.

Locheen—— !

THEOPHILA.

Wait! you haven't heard. [*She changes her position, sitting beside him ; he not responsive, almost shrinking from her.*] Alec—Alec dear—[*leaning her head against his shoulder*]—I intend to be good in the future, so very good.

FRASER.

What do you mean—good?

THEOPHILA.

I intend to get on well with you, wherever we may be—I *will* get on well with you. I've been babyish and silly all my life ; I'm seven-and-twenty ; I'm an old woman ; I've sown my wild oats now.

FRASER.

Wild oats?

THEOPHILA.

Forty-four pounds to the bushel. And so, directly we've fought our way—oh, my, it will be a fight, too!—directly we've fought our way through the Season in London, we'll be off to Locheen——

FRASER.

The Season—here——!

THEOPHILA.

Yes.

FRASER.

Theophila, there will be no Season for us in London, and no Locheen even for me, for two or three years at least. [*Rising.*] We're going abroad——

THEOPHILA.

Abroad——

FRASER.

Directly, directly. There will be only to-morrow to settle everything, to make all arrangements. [*Pacing up and down.*] The servants at Lennox Gardens will be discharged, the house let furnished —perhaps it would be better to let Marlers sell the furniture, and have done with it. [*Pausing in his walk.*] I am returning to Lennox Gardens now, at once ; will you come back with me, or dine with your people and let me fetch you later on ? [*She sits staring at him, without speaking.*] Theo, please let me know your wishes.

THEOPHILA.

[*Quietly.*] No, no—you mustn't do this.

FRASER.

Why not?

THEOPHILA.

Why, don't you see? We've *got* to sit tight here in town; we've *got* to do it, to win back my good name. [FRASER *agitatedly resumes his walk.*] Of course, we shall be asked nowhere, but we must be seen about together, you and I, wherever it's possible for us to squeeze ourselves. [*Rapidly and excitedly.*] There's the Opera ; we can subscribe for a box on the ground tier—the stalls can't help picking you out there. And there we must sit, laughing and talking, Alec, and *convince* people that we're a happy couple and that you believe in me implicitly. And when the Season's done with, *then* Locheen ; we must have Locheen crowded with the best we can lay hands on—many that wouldn't touch me with the tongs at this moment will be glad of a cheap week or two at Locheen in the autumn. And we must let 'em all see that I'm a rattling good indoor, as well as outdoor, wife, and that you're frightfully devoted to me, and that what *she* charged me with— well, simply couldn't have been. And afterwards they'll go back to town and chatter, and in the end the thing will blow over, and—and—— Oh, but to go abroad *now!* [*Going to him and slipping her arm through his.*] Alec, dear old boy, how could you dream of cutting and running *now?*

[*He withdraws his arm.*

FRASER.

Theophila, I—I am sorry to distress you—if it does distress you, but I—I've quite made up my mind. [*Passionately.*] We are going abroad.

THEOPHILA.

I'll not stir !

FRASER.

Would you let me go alone ?

THEOPHILA.

[*Recoiling.*] Oh——

FRASER.

[*Following her.*] You see, you will have to come with me.

THEOPHILA.

You'd be a brute to do it, Alec ! [*Stamping her foot.*] Don't you hear me ? Can't you understand me ? You're not a fool ! I tell you we've got to try to convince people——

FRASER.

People ! People shall not see me play-acting——

THEOPHILA.

Play-acting——

FRASER.

Yes, before I go among people, to try to convince *them,* I have to try to convince *myself.*

THEOPHILA.

What!

FRASER.

[*Sitting.*]   People ! people !
   [*There is silence; she slowly retreats from
   him.*

THEOPHILA.

You—you think there's some—some truth in it,
then ? [*He makes no answer.*]˙ It's true, you
believe ?

FRASER.

I want time—I want time——

THEOPHILA.

Time ?

FRASER.

To shake it off.

THEOPHILA.

To shake it off ?

FRASER.

It was awful in Court.

THEOPHILA.

[*Partly to herself.*] Awful.

FRASER:

As you say, her counsel twisted and turned everything about so.   When he cross-examined you to-
day, and made you say . . . and then the judge
. . . the benefit of the doubt . . . awful . . .

THEOPHILA.

[*Under her breath.*] I see.

FRASER.

[*Rising.*] Yes—that we must go away and be, quietly, together. For the present, there's something even more important than regaining the good opinion of others—there is *ourselves.* Will you come back to Lennox Gardens now, or shall I return for you by and by ?

THEOPHILA.

[*Mechanically.*] By and by.

FRASER.

[*Going to the door.*] Nine o'clock ? or ten ?

THEOPHILA.

Nine or ten.

FRASER.

Which ?

THEOPHILA.

It doesn't matter. [*He goes out. For a few moments she remains quite still ; then she rouses herself, and, with a blank look, wanders about, her arms moving restlessly. Suddenly she presses her hands to her brow and sinks into a chair, with a low half-cry, half-moan.*] Oh ! Oh ! [*After a short burst of crying she examines her wedding-ring, removes it from her finger, and, giving a little laugh, flings it on to the settee. Then she rises,*

*and with an air of determination goes to the writ-
ing table.*] Very well ! Very well !

> [*She sits before the writing table and writes
> rapidly. At intervals she utters an ex-
> clamation ; then sings as she writes.
> The doors are opened, and* HORTON
> *enters.*

HORTON.

[*Collecting the tea-cups.*] Beg pardon, ma'am !

THEOPHILA.

[*Writing.*] Mr. Fraser has gone out, hasn't
he ?

HORTON.

He have, ma'am.

> [HORTON *places the tea-cups on the tea tray,
> lifts up the tray, and is about to carry
> it out.*

THEOPHILA.

Oh, Horton, what became of the bonnet and
cape I came in with ?

HORTON.

[*Looking off.*] Mrs. Emptage lay them down in
the next room. Here they are, ma'am.

THEOPHILA.

Just give them to me. [HORTON *goes off and*

immediately returns with the bonnet, cape, and gloves.] Thanks.

[HORTON *arranges the cape over the back of a chair, places the bonnet and gloves on the table, and withdraws. Having finished her letter and addressed an envelope, she rises and searches for her wedding-ring: finding this she slips it into the letter, and fastens the envelope. Then, keeping the letter in her hand, she puts on her bonnet and cape, standing before the mirror.* SIR FLETCHER *enters, looking disturbed and dejected;* CLAUDE *follows, downcast, silent, and morose, and walks about aimlessly, staring at the carpet.*

SIR FLETCHER PORTWOOD.

[*Discovering* THEOPHILA.] Oh, going out, my dear?

THEOPHILA.

I want a little walk—alone.

SIR FLETCHER PORTWOOD.

To walk it off, eh? [*Ruffling his hair.*] I find I can't walk it off; I've been into the Euston Road; I don't think I can be well. Fortunately, I have a box of most remarkable pills at my chambers. They are prepared by Gilliburton of 88 Piccadilly. Don't forget the number—eighty-eight. Two eights. That's my system of artificial memory. Eighty-eight—two eights.

THEOPHILA.

[*Going to him and kissing him, leaning across the settee.*] Good-bye, uncle.

SIR FLETCHER PORTWOOD.

We shall meet again by and by, dear. I shall dine here quietly, after all.

THEOPHILA.

[*Going to* CLAUDE, *kissing him.*] Good-bye.

CLAUDE.

Oh, you'll see me at dinner too.

THEOPHILA.

[*Handing him the letter.*] Give that to 'Tina, will you ? Claude—take care of mother.

CLAUDE.

[*Mildly surprised.*] Take care of mother !

THEOPHILA.

Yes, be a good boy, and look after her. Ta, ta!
[*She goes out.*

CLAUDE.

Boy ! *my* boyhood is long past. [*Pinching the envelope.*] There's coin in this—money.

SIR FLETCHER PORTWOOD.

[*Sitting on the settee, fatigued.*] Eh ? Don't forget, Claude—Gilliburton. Think of Gilly, corruption of Gilbert. Gilbert, a well-known sculptor—or writer ; I forget which. Burton,

man I jobbed two horses from—bays—Burton.
There you have Gilly and Burton—Gilliburton.
My own system of mnemonics. *Memoria technica.*

CLAUDE.

It's not a coin ; it's a ring.

SIR FLETCHER PORTWOOD.

[*Irritably.*] What are you talking about, my
boy ? You always appear to be masticating some
commonplace or other.

HORTON *appears.*

HORTON.

Beg pardon, Sir Fletcher. Mrs. Cloys wants to
wish you good-day, Sir Fletcher. I wasn't aware
where you was, Sir Fletcher.

CLAUDE.

[*Giving the letter to* HORTON.] Miss Justina.
[HORTON *withdraws.*

SIR FLETCHER PORTWOOD.

[*Rising.*] I'd quite forgotten your aunt. Do,
please, look unconcerned, Claude. Let her see that
men can display courage and decision at such
moments.

[*Humming an air, he unbuttons his coat
and throws it back, sticking his thumbs
in his waistcoat pockets. Some news-
papers fall from the breast of his coat ;
he is hastily picking them up when*
MRS. CLOYS *enters.*

SIR FLETCHER PORTWOOD.

[*Meekly.*]   You are going, Harriet?

MRS. CLOYS.

Fletcher, you've been out to buy evening papers!

SIR FLETCHER PORTWOOD.

[*Putting them into his tail pockets.*]   The malicious utterances of the judge are not in these editions.

MRS. CLOYS.

I thought you never——!

SIR FLETCHER PORTWOOD.

It is somebody's duty to overlook the reports of this case.   I see that one vile placard announces, " Lively cross-examination of Mrs. Fraser."

MRS. CLOYS.

Lively !

SIR FLETCHER PORTWOOD.

[*Producing a newspaper.*]   Here's a rag which dares to give illustrations—" Sketches in Court."

MRS. CLOYS.

Have you contrived to get among them?

SIR FLETCHER PORTWOOD.

[*Opening the paper.*]   I happen to *be* among them.   But the fool of an artist has completely missed my salient points——

JUSTINA *runs in with* THEOPHILA'S *letter, opened, and the wedding-ring.*

JUSTINA.

Aunt! oh, I say! What do you think?
Theo's gone.

SIR FLETCHER PORTWOOD.

She's gone out for a walk.   [*To* MRS. CLOYS.]
Here it is.   That's from an old photograph ; I
don't wear that sort of collar *now.*

JUSTINA.

[*Advancing between* MRS. CLOYS *and* SIR
FLETCHER.]   What are you talking about?   Look
here ! [*Reading.*]   "'Tina, hand enclosed to my
husband when he comes back for me to-night
after dinner." [*Showing the ring.*]   It's her wedding-ring. [*Reading.*]   "He believes that what
that creature charged me with is true, and wants
to take me away and hide me.   All is up with me.
Oh, those pipers at Locheen are playing into my
brain again.   Good-bye all.—THEO. P. S.—Jack
Allingham would not treat a woman so like dirt."

MRS. CLOYS.

[*Agitatedly.*]   I can't hear you.   [*Taking the
letter from* JUSTINA.]   Let me see it.

JUSTINA.

What shall we do?   We must do something.
Uncle !

SIR FLETCHER PORTWOOD.

[*Confused.*]   We must certainly do something,
at once.   Er—it *is* her wedding-ring, I suppose ?

JUSTINA.

[*Impatiently.*] Oh——! Aunt!

SIR FLETCHER PORTWOOD.

[*Encountering* CLAUDE.] Don't stand there,
Claude, looking precisely like an owl.

MRS. CLOYS.

[*Returning the letter* to JUSTINA.] Jump into
a cab ; you must take that to Mr. Fraser.

JUSTINA.

[*Hurrying to the door.*] All right. [*Pausing.*]
What shall I do if I don't find him at home ?

SIR FLETCHER PORTWOOD.

If, if, if ! Why throw obstacles ?

JUSTINA.

I'm not throwing them. I merely say, what if
he's out, or hasn't gone back to Lennox Gardens
at all ?

SIR FLETCHER PORTWOOD.

This is a moment for action !

CLAUDE.

[*Sitting at the writing-table.*] Ha, ha ! what a
hideous mockery the whole world is ! Life——!

SIR FLETCHER PORTWOOD.

Let us have none of your sickening optimism,
sir ! and in the presence of your aunt and sister!

MRS. CLOYS.

[*Holding out her hand for the letter.*]   Show it
to me again.   [JUSTINA *brings the letter to* MRS.
CLOYS, *who begins reading.*]   "Hand enclosed to
my husband when he comes back for me to-night
after dinner."

JUSTINA.

Ten or eleven o'clock.   Where on earth will
she be by ten or eleven o'clock?

SIR FLETCHER PORTWOOD.

[*Going to the door.*]   I'll tell her mother——

JUSTINA.

[*Intercepting him.*]   For goodness' sake, not
yet.   Mother's no use.

MRS. CLOYS.

[*Reading.*]   "P. S.—Jack Allingham would not
treat a woman so like dirt."   Jack Allingham——
[*Suddenly*] Justina!   [JUSTINA *again comes to
her.*]   There's only one very great danger.

JUSTINA.

Why, you don't think Theo would—take poison
—or——!

MRS. CLOYS.

No, I mean a worse danger than that.   [*Pointing to a sentence in the letter.*]   That one.

JUSTINA.

[*Reading.*]   "Jack Allingham would not treat a
woman——"   [*Staring at* MRS. CLOYS.]   Oh——!

MRS. CLOYS.

This Mr. Allingham? Exceedingly kind and gentle to women—is that the class of man he belongs to?

JUSTINA.

Y—yes.

MRS. CLOYS.

Suppose—suppose this wretched girl lets her mind dwell too much just now on Mr. Allingham's —kindness!

JUSTINA.

Aunt!

MRS. CLOYS.

[*Again returning the letter to* JUSTINA—*with decision.*] Where does he live? Where is he likely to be found?

JUSTINA.

It's in the Red Book. [*Pointing to the writing-table.*] Claude——

SIR FLETCHER PORTWOOD.

Bring me the Red Book! [CLAUDE *finds the Red Book; he and* SIR FLETCHER PORTWOOD *search for the address.*] Allingham—A—A—A— [*Finding the letter.*] A!

CLAUDE.

You're looking at " Ashley Gardens "——
[MRS. CLOYS *and* JUSTINA *join* SIR FLETCHER PORTWOOD *and* CLAUDE *impatiently.*

JUSTINA.

I know it's there.   He went into lodgings when he parted from her.   And he has a little cottage in Surrey——

CLAUDE.

[*Finding the name.*]   " Allingham——! "

SIR FLETCHER PORTWOOD.

[*Taking the book from him.*]   " Allingham, John Crawshaw, Esq., 11 Bentham Street, W., and Turf and Garrick Clubs. — The Lichens, Epsom, Surrey."

> [MRS. CLOYS *takes the book from* SIR FLETCHER.   *She tears out the page and throws the book upon the settee.*

MRS. CLOYS.

[*Folding the extracted page, and slipping it into her glove.*]   Fletcher, Claude, you had better come with me.   I may want you both.   Claude, whistle a four-wheeled cab.   You hear me !

> [CLAUDE *goes out.*

SIR FLETCHER PORTWOOD.

But, Harriet, do you seriously, soberly, entertain the notion ?

MRS. CLOYS.

Get your hat !   [SIR FLETCHER *goes out.*   MRS. CLOYS *turns to* JUSTINA.]   Telegraph to the Bishop of St. Olpherts, The Palace, St. Olpherts : " Detained here to-night.   Return, D. V., forenoon to-morrow. Get to bed early. Affectionate messages.—H."

[*The sound of a cab-whistle, twice or thrice repeated, is heard.*

JUSTINA.

" Detained here to-night. Return forenoon to-morrow——"

MRS. CLOYS.

" D. V."

JUSTINA.

" D. V. Go to bed early——"

MRS. CLOYS.

Say, " Be in bed by eleven."

JUSTINA.

Yes. " Love——"

MRS. CLOYS.

No, no—" Affectionate messages."

JUSTINA.

" Affectionate messages.—H."

MRS. CLOYS.

Thank you.

JUSTINA.

Aunt ! When I see Alec Fraser, am I to say anything—about what you are doing ?

MRS. CLOYS.

For mercy's sake, don't put any idea into his

head that isn't there already !   Not a word to a
soul——   .

CLAUDE *appears in the doorway, hat in hand.*

CLAUDE.

Cab, aunt.   .

MRS. CLOYS.

I'm coming.   [CLAUDE *withdraws.*]   Not a
word, except that we've gone out, blindly, to try
and find her.

JUSTINA.

Wait ! you must tell me ; do you suspect that
Theophila is—guilty ?

MRS. CLOYS.

[*Looking at her steadily.*]   Woman, what do
you suspect ?

JUSTINA.

[*Falteringly.*]   Then I can't understand you.

MRS. CLOYS.

Why not, pray ?

JUSTINA.

I've always taken you for one of those who pick
up their skirts and stalk away as far as possible
from this kind of thing.

MRS. CLOYS.

Ah, you don't—[*moved*]—oh, my dear !

JUSTINA.

What ?

Mrs. Cloys.

You don't know what was really at the bottom of all my quarrels with your mother. I've no children. I'd have given the world if Theo had been mine.

Justina.

[*A little bitterly.*] · Theo ! Theo !

Mrs. Cloys.

[*Taking her by the shoulder, almost shaking her.*] You, too ! [*Kissing her.*] Bless you, you'd have been better than nothing !

[*She goes out.* Justina *stands, her lips parted, staring into space.*

END OF THE FIRST ACT.

THE SECOND ACT.

The Scene represents a room in MR. ALLINGHAM'S
. *cottage at Epsom. On the left-hand side is a
fireplace, with a fire burning ; above this is a
door giving on to the hall ; while below it is
a similar door, over which hangs a portière,
drawn aside, admitting to the dining-room.
Facing us is a large open French window ;
and beyond is a view of a pretty garden with
trees, laurels, etc. On the right, also facing
us, but nearer, are a few balustered steps leading to an arched opening which is about three
feet from the ground. The opening, across
which runs a rod supporting a portière, admits
to a small room, which, although containing
no books that are visible, is called the library.
All the furniture and accessories are characteristic of a well-to-do bachelor's residence. It
is twilight.*

DENZIL SHAFTO *and* PETER ELPHICK, *two well-
groomed, smart-looking men of about five-and-
thirty, dressed for dinner, are shown in by*
QUAIFE, *a manservant.* QUAIFE *is carrying
a banjo in a case.*

SHAFTO.
What time did Mr. Allingham get down ?

QUAIFE.

[*Placing the banjo on the table.*] Half an hour ago, sir; I'm now dressing him. [*To* ELPHICK.] Glad you brought the banjo, Mr. Elphick.

ELPHICK.

[*A heavy-looking man with staring eyes—taking the banjo from its case with great care.*] Nearly made me lose the train, Quaife, puzzlin' whether to bring it or not.

QUAIFE.

[*Laying the case aside.*] Do Mr. Allingham a load of good, sir—a little melody after dinner.

SHAFTO.

Mr. Allingham rather fatigued ?

QUAIFE.

Never saw him so played out, sir. [*Closing the windows.*] Oh, Mr. Allingham's compliments, Mr. Shafto, and he says he forgot to inquire whether you and Mr. Elphick would sleep at The Lichens to-night.

SHAFTO.

Not to-night, thanks. I've arranged to take Mr. Elphick on to my father's place at Leatherhead.

ELPHICK.

We shan't keep you up here till the last train, Quaife, or anything like. Dessay Mr. Allingham 'll be glad to turn in early.

QUAIFE.

Not much good *him* turning in, Mr. Elphick.

SHAFTO.

Queer nights lately, of sorts?

QUAIFE.

Shockin', Mr. Shafto.   [QUAIFE *goes out.*

SHAFTO.

[*Looking around.*] Here we are again, Peter.

ELPHICK.

'Pears so.

SHAFTO.

[*Wandering about.*] This is my first visit to this box since Jack came back here after his split with his wife.

ELPHICK.

And mine ; thought he'd sold it.

SHAFTO.

He merely let it, when he married—let it to a stockbroker. Peter, Jack must have had some sort of a premonition——

ELPHICK.

Some sort of what?

SHAFTO.

Premonition——

ELPHICK.

Stoopid ass of a word.

SHAFTO.

Some sort of a premonition of his speedy return
to single life. [*Looking out of the window.*]
Same spotless white gate, I rejoice to see ; same
elms ; same laurels—— [*Ascending the steps.*]
The library—— [*Entering the room.*] My heart
sinks within me. [*From within.*] No, by Jove !
Peter ! Peter !

[ELPHICK *goes and looks into the room
through the balustrade.*

ELPHICK.

What's wrong ?

SHAFTO.

[*From within.*] Nothing. I breathe again.
All the essential features of Jack's library are
undisturbed. [*Coming down the steps.*] A lux-
urious sofa, Ruff's Turf Guide, and the Stud Book.

ELPHICK.

[*Drearily.*] Blessed if there's anything to make
fun of in that.

SHAFTO.

[*At a table examining bottles.*] Delightful !
Same soda water, same——

ELPHICK.

[*Sitting, nursing his banjo.*] No, hang it !

SHAFTO.

[*Pouring out a glass of Vermouth.*] Vermouth.
Peter, I was totting up things this morning, gently
and quietly, in my bath.

ELPHICK.

[*Blowing a speck of dust from his banjo.*]   Not really ?

SHAFTO.

[*Seriously.*]   Yes.   You weren't at Jack's weddin' ?

ELPHICK.

No, I was up at Mahabaleshwar that spring with Sandington.   You stood best man, didn't you ?

SHAFTO.

I did.   And look here—Jack Allingham is the seventh I've been best man to in nine years.

ELPHICK.

[*Abstractedly.*]   Good figgers.

SHAFTO.

[*Frowning.*]   And they've all managed to get into the Divorce Court since, one way or another. *After a pause.*]   How's that ?

ELPHICK.

Good figgers.

JOHN ALLINGHAM *enters, a simple, boyish man, of about thirty, looking pale and worn.   He is dressed for dinner.*

JOHN.

[*Shaking hands with* SHAFTO.]   Halloa, Denzil ! [*To* ELPHICK, *shaking hands with him.*]   Well, Peter !   It's awfully good of you fellows proposing to see me through this evening.

ELPHICK.

Not in the least.

SHAFTO.

Speak for yourself, Peter.

JOHN.

I couldn't have endured my own company to-night, I can tell you. Sorry you can't sleep here, though.

SHAFTO.

My governor hasn't seen Peter since he's been home this leave. It's an old promise——

JOHN.

I understand. [*Taking the banjo from* ELPHICK.] And you've actually brought the banjo.

ELPHICK.

Well, when a man's a bit low, sometimes a little music——

JOHN.

Thanks. [*To both of them.*] Warm, yesterday and to-day, in that Law Court, wasn't it?

ELPHICK.

Agra in June.

JOHN.

Warm in every sense of the word, eh?

SHAFTO.

Hell.

JOHN.

[*With his hand to his brow.*] Gur-r-r-h!

SHAFTO.

[*Sharply.*]   Now then ?

ELPHICK.

It's done with now.

JOHN.

[*Recovering himself.*]   True ; that cursed night-mare of an approaching trial isn't waiting for me upstairs, in that bedroom of mine, any longer. And to-morrow morning I shall wake with a start to find—what 'll the feeling be like !—that I've no lawyers to interview.   Besides, I haven't much to complain of.   You two fellows have kept close at my elbow through the whole business—hardly ever left me.   Well, that's friendship—[*shaking hands abruptly, first with* ELPHICK, *then with* SHAFTO]—God bless yer !

> [*He walks away and sits on the settee, look-ing into the fire.* ELPHICK *and* SHAFTO *stand together, eyeing him uneasily.*

SHAFTO.

[*In a whisper, to* ELPHICK.]   Peter, our bags are here.   What d'ye say to not leaving him to-night, after all ?

ELPHICK.

[*In a whisper.*]   Yes, I don't suppose your guv'-nor wants to see me so desperate bad as all that comes to.

SHAFTO.

No, I don't suppose he does—I mean, we can go over in the morning.

JOHN.

[*Looking up.*] Eh ?

SHAFTO.

Nothing.

JOHN.

[*Passing his fingers over the strings of the banjo.*] You don't remember, Denzil—nor you, Peter, I suppose ; *she* used to thrum on this thing —well, hardly this thing—the guitar—much the same. Oh, yes, she used to play it very nicely.

SHAFTO.

[*Puzzled.*] Who? Mrs. Fraser?

JOHN.

Mrs. Fraser ! No ! [*Handling the banjo roughly.*] My wife.

ELPHICK.

[*Hurrying across to John, taking the banjo from him.*] Excuse me, old feller.

JOHN.

[*Starting up.*] I was close to her to-day ; we stared each other right in the eyes. We didn't mean to—we simply did it. We met in the cor- ridor during lunch-time ; I was getting out of the way of old Portwood ; I turned sharply—and there we were, my wife and I, face to face. It might have been for ten seconds—it was like an hour.

ELPHICK.

Did she look angry ?

JOHN.

No. Downright ill and distressed. [*To both
of them.*] You've seen her in Court?

SHAFTO.

Yes.

ELPHICK.

Yes.

JOHN.

Yesterday?

SHAFTO.

We said "How d'ye do" to her yesterday.

ELPHICK.

We told you.

JOHN.

Oh, yes. To-day?

SHAFTO.

Not to speak to.

ELPHICK.

She nodded to us this morning from the—what
do they call it?—not the sink——

SHAFTO.

Well.

ELPHICK.

Well of the Court.

JOHN.

Denzil.

SHAFTO.

'Ullo?

JOHN.

She was very pretty when I married her, wasn't she ?

SHAFTO.

Undoubtedly.

[JOHN *sits leaning his head upon his hands.*
SHAFTO *walks away, quietly, to the
window.* ELPHICK *sits on the settee,
and, turning his face to the fire, strikes
up a tune on his banjo.*

JOHN.

That's right ! tune up, Peter ! If I had a savage breast this evening you might soothe it with your Tinka-tinka-tinka-tinka-tink, as Kipling says. But I haven't—isn't that odd ? Boys, do you know, all the bitterness I've been feeling towards her seems to have died out of me ; and she's been dragging me pretty thoroughly through the mud lately. Isn't that odd ?

SHAFTO.

[*Leaving the window and coming to the back of
settee.*] Well, she's lost the day, you see.

ELPHICK.

[*Ceasing playing.*] She's beaten ; got nothin' for her pains.

JOHN.

I suppose that's it. Ah, but her face ! I hadn't seen it for months. And the silence between us was so strange.

SHAFTO.

Yes, there wasn't much of *that*, old chap, between you two when you were together.

JOHN.

No; *didn't* we quarrel! And yet, this morning, during our little deadly-silent encounter, she seemed to say more to me than she'd ever said in her life before. By Jove, she *has* suffered—[*starting up*]—oh, d—— it!

[*He paces to and fro;* ELPHICK *hurriedly resumes his playing.*

SHAFTO.

[*Seating himself on the back of the settee, speaking with a drawl.*] Ah, I shouldn't worry myself too much, if I were you, about that. Other people have suffered.

JOHN.

[*Pausing in his walk.*] Mrs. Fraser——?

SHAFTO.

[*Indifferently.*] Oh, she amongst 'em.

JOHN.

[*In a low voice.*] Poor little Theo Fraser! I'm forgetting her.

SHAFTO.

Forget all round, my dear Jack—that's the ticket; for the future, cultivate a single-minded devotion to yourself——

JOHN.

And the horses ! You're right, Denzil. By the bye, I had a line from O'Halligan yesterday— where is it ? [*Going to a writing-table and rummaging among the litter there.*] He fancies Kildaowen very strongly. The mare's feeding well ; that's always been their difficulty, you know——

SHAFTO.

[*Quietly, looking towards the window.*] Jack.

JOHN.

Eh ?

SHAFTO.

Who's that woman out there ?

[ELPHICK *ceases playing.*

JOHN.

Where ?

SHAFTO.

In your garden.

[JOHN *looks towards the window ;* ELPHICK *rises and makes one of the group.*

JOHN.

[*After a pause.*] I don't see anybody.

SHAFTO.

She's behind the laurels now.

JOHN.

[*About to go to the window.*] One of the maids——

SHAFTO.

[*Laying his hand on* JOHN's *arm.*] Wait a bit.
[*Goes cautiously to the window, peeps out, and
comes away.*] I say, old chap.

JOHN.

What's the matter?

SHAFTO.

I thought so. It's your wife. [*There is a
moment's pause, then an excited movement from*
JOHN.] Stop! [*A pause.*] What are you going
to do?

JOHN.

[*Dazed.*] Do! . . . . do! . . . .

SHAFTO.

Not anything stoopid, Jack?

JOHN.

[*Excitedly.*] Clear out for a minute, you two
fellows.

> [SHAFTO *goes up the steps and into the
> library, drawing the portière across the
> door as he disappears.*

JOHN.

Get out, Peter!

ELPHICK.

[*Going up the steps and pausing at the door.*]
Jack.

JOHN.

What is it?

Elphick.

[*With an empty expression of face and voice.*]
Don't do anything weak.

John.

Get out ! [Elphick *disappears.* John *hurriedly glances round the room and arranges a displaced chair. Then he discovers that* Elphick *has left the banjo upon the settee, and he seizes it impatiently.*] Oh—— [*Going to the door of the library and drawing aside the portière.*] Here ! Peter ! catch ! [*He throws the banjo into the room, and readjusts the portière. The instrument is heard to fall with a crash to the floor. He looks into the library, hastily.*] I beg your pardon, old fellow. [*He descends the steps and goes to the window and opens it, speaking in a low voice.*] Is anyone there ? [*A pause.*] Someone's there.

Olive.

[*From a little distance.*]   Yes.

John.

Who is it ?

Olive.

Olive.

John.

[*Sternly.*]   Well ?

Olive.

Are you by yourself ?

JOHN.

Yes. [*After a pause.*]   Come in.

[*He draws back to allow her to pass him.
After a short delay she enters, and,
without looking at him, comes right
into the room.   He closes the window,
but remains at that end of the room.
OLIVE ALLINGHAM is a fashionably
and richly dressed woman of a little
over thirty years of age—pale, worn,
red-eyed, but still handsome.   In manner she is alternately beseeching and
gentle, angry and imperious.   The
twilight now gradually deepens into
dusk.*

OLIVE.

You have some men here?

JOHN.

Shafto and Peter Elphick.   I asked them to
clear out for a moment.

OLIVE.

What will they think?

JOHN.

[*With a shrug of the shoulder.*]   They can
scarcely know what to think.

OLIVE.

[*Walking to the mantelpiece.*]   What do you
think yourself, of my humbling myself in this

fashion ? [*Turning to him.*] What do you——?
[*As she has crossed to the left of the room, he, still
at a distance, has moved over to the right. Speaking with a catch in her breath.*] Oh, don't do
that! I'm not poisonous, John. [*He approaches
stiffly and silently. She advances towards him
plaintively.*] John, I am quite worn out—[*putting her hand to her bosom*]—burnt out here.
This desperate lawsuit has been my last bolt. I'm
finished—spent. I know my regrets won't avail
us much at this time of day ; the future has a
most melancholy look-out for both of us ; but I
want to tell you I am truly conscious, at last, of
the evil my jealousy has wrought. [*Sitting
weakly.*] John, I—I am quite reasonable at last.

[QUAIFE *enters.*

QUAIFE.

Dinner is s——
[*He breaks off, staring at* OLIVE.

OLIVE.

Good-evening, Quaife.

QUAIFE.

[*Aghast.*] Good-evening, ma'am.

JOHN.

[*To* QUAIFE.] Tell Mrs. Quaife to delay dinner
for—for——

OLIVE.

[*Rising and turning away—in an altered tone.*]
Oh, five minutes—ten at the outside.

JOHN.

For a quarter of an hour. [*Sharply.*] The lamps.

[QUAIFE *withdraws, as if in a dream.*

OLIVE.

[*Bitterly.*] I much regret keeping you and your friends from your dinner. It's an exceptionally elaborate entertainment to-night, I suppose?

JOHN.

No, no; it's of no consequence——

OLIVE.

Dinner! dinner! If every woman in the world was weeping her heart out, men would be found dining—feeding—feasting! What was I saying when Quaife blundered in? Where was I?

JOHN.

[*Looking at her steadily.*] Quite reasonable at last.

OLIVE.

[*After a brief pause, speaking gently again.*] Oh, John——! [*Advancing a few steps.*] It was inconsiderate of me to break out in that way. But I don't mean half the brutal things I say; I never did.

JOHN.

You couldn't have done so.

OLIVE.

Any jealous woman will tell you what a slave

she is to her paroxysms. Oh, they are dreadful, while they last! [*Agitatedly.*] The flame behind one's eyes, the buzzing in the ears, the dry tongue, the thumping of the heart—— [*Calming herself, breathlessly.*] Thank God, I'm cured!

JOHN.

You've said something like this to me on other occasions.

OLIVE.

Never under such extraordinary circumstances. [*Going to him.*] The fact that I can drag myself to you, in this spirit, after my defeat, for the sake of a few words with you, must show you what an altered woman I am. [*Sitting.*] John, I felt I couldn't go back to that lonely flat of mine to-night without first proving to you how thorough my remorse is. [*Looking round.*] That dismal flat! [*In an altered tone.*] You appear to be extremely comfortable here.

JOHN.

Oh, it's a little place—very cramped——

OLIVE.

This is where you gave me and papa tea once, when we were engaged to be married.

JOHN.

I remember.

OLIVE.

And now—— [*Excitedly.*] Ha, I suppose I'm a fool not to indulge myself just as luxuriously,

just us—— [*She meets his eye and breaks off*
shamefacedly. Faltering, with her hand to her
brow.] Where was I—again?

JOHN.

You were engaged in demonstrating how
thorough · your remorse is.

OLIVE.

Oh, yes. [*Weakly.*] After the case ended this
afternoon I walked about the streets quite light-
headed, till I summoned up resolution to try to
find you. [*With an effort.*] John, that—that
lady——

JOHN.

What lady ?

OLIVE.

[*Agitatedly.*] Mrs. Fraser of Locheen.

JOHN.

Yes?

OLIVE.

[*Repressing her agitation.*] Of course, the
judge fully justified my action by the very
severe way he spoke of her.

JOHN.

His remarks were infamous ! I could have
taken him by the throat and thrown him into the
body of the Court. No right-thinking person
would have blamed me for doing so.

OLIVE.

However, he gave' her the benefit of the doubt——

JOHN.

[*Scornfully.*] The benefit of the doubt !

OLIVE.

And paid me the compliment of believing that I would, as one woman to another, prefer such a course being adopted.

JOHN.

[*Pacing to and fro.*] Poor, wretched little Mrs. Fraser !

OLIVE.

Wait ! Even *I* see the injustice of it.

JOHN.

[*Eagerly.*] You do ?

OLIVE.

Haven't I told you I am reasonable at last ? For whether she be innocent or guilty is no longer the question.

JOHN.

I'm glad that is no longer the question !

OLIVE.

The point is, this woman is entitled to the benefit of the doubt. [*Rising and walking to and fro.*] But how can she ever receive the benefit of the doubt if those words, which imply the doubt, are always to hang over her ?

JOHN.

That's it !

OLIVE.

And they will hang over her—for ever.

JOHN.

For ever.

OLIVE.

For ever. [*Turning to him.*] Unless I cancel them—remove them.

JOHN.

You !

OLIVE.

I could, John—by my attitude towards her in public—in society.

JOHN.

[*Staring at her.*] Why, certainly you could.

OLIVE.

[*Leaning over a chair and speaking almost into his ear.*] Would you like me to ?

JOHN.

Like you to !

OLIVE.

I want to atone to you, if I can, in some measure, for the suffering I've caused you.   Would you like me to right Mrs. Fraser ?

JOHN.

Oh, Olive !——

OLIVE.

John !

JOHN.

[*With emotion.*] If you were always so generous—so good !

OLIVE.

[*Drawing back suddenly.*] Ah !

JOHN.

[*After a brief pause.*] I've offended you by
saying that.

OLIVE.

[*In a hard voice.*] You are evidently very keen
concerning her.

JOHN.

[*Blankly.*] Keen !

OLIVE.

She's a vulgar, common little thing, I'm afraid.

JOHN.

That's not true.

OLIVE.

Her people are common—excessively bad tone.

JOHN.

Her people are now her husband's people. She
is married to a gentleman.

OLIVE.

Mr. Fraser has been away from her as much as

possible—[*her eyes flashing*]—*you* know that
better than anybody.

JOHN.

[*Indignantly.*] Why do you come here—after
all our struggles and failures, after the injury
you've endeavoured to do me? Why do you
torture me, and insult me, by trying to repeat the
old heart-breaking scenes?

> [*He throws himself into a chair distractedly.
> There is a pause; then she slowly goes
> to a chair, drags it towards him, and
> sits beside him.*

OLIVE.

[*Panting.*] Torture *you?* Oh! oh, I suffer
too! [*Rocking herself to and fro.*] Well, there
can be no punishment for jealous women in
another world; we are d——d in this.

JOHN.

[*In a muffled voice, with his head on his hands.*]
And the fire has burnt out in you, you tell me!

OLIVE.

I suppose the cinders still retain a little heat.
dear.

JOHN.

[*Brokenly.*] Dear! . . . . dear! . . . .

OLIVE.

Yes. I know my actions are contradictory,
but—[*her hand stealing towards his*]—in my heart,

John—always—in my heart—— [*The banjo suddenly strikes up an air.* JOHN *and* OLIVE *raise
their heads and stare at each other ; then* OLIVE
*slowly backs her chair to its original position.
Speaking in a whisper.*] What's that?

JOHN.

Peter.

OLIVE.

Peter——!

JOHN.

He brought his banjo with him.

OLIVE.

[*Aghast.*] Why—— ! . . . Oh !

JOHN.

[*Blankly.*] Eh ?

OLIVE.

If *we* hear the banjo with such distinctness——
[*They rise. He hurriedly ascends the steps
and disappears through the portière.
The music of the banjo stops abruptly,
and the sound of voices comes from the
library.* QUAIFE *enters, carrying a
lamp which he deposits on the table ;
then, always watching* OLIVE, *he lights
the standard-lamp and draws the window curtains.*

SHAFTO.

My dear fellow——!

ELPHICK.

My dear Jack——!

JOHN.

S-s-sh !

SHAFTO.

You might have remembered——

JOHN.

S-s-sh ! s-s-sh ! [*The voices in the library are hushed.*

OLIVE.

[*Commanding herself and crossing to the fire-place.*]　And how are you, Quaife ?

QUAIFE.

Very well indeed, I thank you, ma'am.

OLIVE.

And your wife ?

QUAIFE.

Exceedingly healthy, ma'am, for a stout person.

OLIVE.

I hope you look after Mr. Allingham thoroughly, all of you.

QUAIFE.

[*Dropping his voice impressively.*]　We regard him as a trust, ma'am, if I may make use of the expression.

OLIVE.

[*Sharply.*]   A what ?

QUAIFE.

A solemn trust, ma'am.

OLIVE.

[*Turning away.*]   Stuff and nonsense !

QUAIFE.

I beg pardon, ma'am, if I have gone too far.

JOHN *returns.*

JOHN.

[*Coming down the steps, a little flustered.*]
Quaife.

QUAIFE.

Sir ?

JOHN.

Er—Mr. Shafto and Mr. Elphick don't dine.

QUAIFE.

Not dine, sir !

JOHN.

They have to go on to Leatherhead at once.   Is
the boy ready to carry their bags to the station ?

QUAIFE.

The boy can be worried till he's ready, sir.

JOHN.

All right.

[QUAIFE *withdraws.* JOHN *and* OLIVE *now
speak in whispers.*

OLIVE.

I don't wish this.

JOHN.

They offered to go ; they'd rather go.

OLIVE.

Have they heard much ?

JOHN.

Er—next to nothing ; a syllable or two when we were sitting there. That's why Peter struck up a tune. [*Laughing a little wildly.*] Ha, ha, ha !

OLIVE.

[*In the same way.*] Ha, ha, ha ! [*Glancing towards the door.*] Shall I slip into the dining-room while they pass out ?

JOHN.

Please don't. They're old friends of both of us ; they understand perfectly——

OLIVE.

[*Returning to the fireplace.*] I'll face it out if you wish it.

JOHN.

[*Calling.*] Denzil! Peter!

> [SHAFTO *and* ELPHICK *sedately emerge from the library and descend the steps.* SHAFTO *bows to* OLIVE.

OLIVE.

[*Advancing, shaking hands with him across the table, graciously.*] Oh, Mr. Shafto, I am so sorry to upset everybody in this way——

SHAFTO.

Not at all. I—ah—we—er—my father—at Leatherhead——　.

> [ELPHICK, *encumbered with his banjo and the banjo-case, joins* SHAFTO. JOHN *goes to the door.*

OLIVE.

[*Shaking hands with* ELPHICK *across the table.*] Why should you lose your dinner? I have really finished all my—my business with my—with—Mr. Allingham.　　　　　　　　　　·

ELPHICK.

[*With an effort, earnestly.*] No you haven't, Mrs. Allingham. Take it up, when we've gone, where you broke off. [*Wringing her hand.*] Do everything you've offered to do ; try and square things——

> [JOHN *comes to him and draws him away towards the door.*

JOHN.

[*To* OLIVE.] Excuse me ; one moment——

> [*The three men go out, leaving* OLIVE *staring before her.* JOHN, SHAFTO, *and* ELPHICK *are heard talking together in the hall.*

JOHN.

[*Outside.*]   My dear Denzil ! my dear Peter——

SHAFTO.

[*Outside.*]   My good fellow, we are not, at present, in the least hungry.

>   [OLIVE *runs up the steps and disappears in the library.*

JOHN.

[*Outside.*]   No conveyance of any kind to get you to the station——

ELPHICK.

[*Outside.*]   Much prefer walking, I assure you.

SHAFTO.

[*Outside.*]   Good-bye.

ELPHICK.

[*Outside.*]   Enjoyed seeing the cottage again enormously.

>   [*The sound of the voices dies away; a clock in the library strikes nine;* JOHN *returns.*

JOHN.

[*Looking round.*]   Olive—Olive——

>   [*She reappears.*

OLIVE.

You didn't tell me the truth.   You can hear the slightest sound in there.

JOHN.

I beg your pardon. Those men went clean out
of my head. I was an ass.

OLIVE.

[*Descending the steps.*] And that idiot offers
me his advice ! Take it up where you broke off !

JOHN.

At least, it's good advice.

OLIVE.

Where *did* we break off ?

JOHN.

At Mrs. Fraser——

OLIVE.

[*Walking up the stage, beating her hands
together.*] Mrs. Fraser ! the eternal Mrs. Fraser !
Oh ! . . . . oh ! . . . . [*Throwing herself into
the chair facing the window.*] I shall be quite
calm in a moment. [*Faintly.*] Those men upset
me.

JOHN.

[*Going to her solicitously.*] To-day has been
as exhausting for you as for the rest of us. Of
course, there's a dinner prepared here——

OLIVE.

[*Quickly, half-frightened.*] Oh, no, dear ; I
couldn't sit down to table with you ; I'm not
entitled to do that. Fetch me a glass of wine and

a biscuit. [*Appealingly.*]   Don't let a servant bring
it, John.   [*He goes to the dining-room door ; she
rises and calls him.*]   John!—[*her head drooping*]—do you think we shall ever sit at the same
table again, you and I ?

JOHN.

[*After a pause, sitting, looking away from her.*]
Oh, Olive, Olive ! remember——!

OLIVE.

[*Fidgeting with the cigarette-box.*]   Not for
many years, of course—three or four years, at
least. - Time makes the oddest things possible.

JOHN.

[*Thoughtfully.*]   I suppose so.

OLIVE.

It would appear supremely ridiculous to the
world, you're afraid ?

JOHN.

Pish ! the world don't matter a d——

OLIVE.

[*Softly.*]   Ah, that's delicious !

JOHN.

What is——?

OLIVE.

I haven't heard a man swear since I turned you
out of Pont Street.   [*Dreamily, almost inaudibly,*

as she plays with a cigarette.] D——! [*He looks round at her ; she is lost in thought ; suddenly she crushes the cigarette, and flings it from her fiercely.*] Ah ! Theo Fraser smokes !

JOHN.

[*Starting up in a rage.*] Hah ! hah !

[*He goes out of the room.*

OLIVE.

[*Following him a few steps, penitently.*] Oh, John !—— [*There is a knock at the door.*] Yes ?

QUAIFE *enters, with some cards on a salver.*

QUAIFE.

[*Looking round.*] I beg pardon, ma'am ; a lady and two gentlemen would like to see Mr. Allingham, if it's not disturbing him.

[*She goes to the table and examines the cards.*

OLIVE.

[*In a hard voice.*] Are these people friends of Mr. Allingham's ? Have they ever called on him before ?

QUAIFE.

No, ma'am. [*Hesitatingly.*] I fancy the eldest of the two gentlemen came once, if not twice, to Pont Street in—in—in your time, ma'am.

OLIVE.

I'll give those to Mr. Allingham. [*He lays the cards out on the table.*] You'll be rung for. [*He *goes towards the door.*] You haven't mentioned that I am here ?

QUAIFE.

Oh, no, ma'am. I simply said Mr. Allingham was engaged for the moment.

OLIVE.

Quite right ; thank you.

> [*He withdraws. She eagerly scrutinises the cards, re-arranges them upon the table, then goes to the fire-place and stands waiting impatiently.* JOHN *re-enters, carrying a decanter of champagne and some biscuits in a silver dish, which he places on a side-table.*

JOHN.

This is the Moet we had just begun to drink when we—— You rather liked it, I fancy.

OLIVE.

Some people have called ; they're waiting to see you.

JOHN.

[*Turning.*] People—so late ?

OLIVE.

[*Pointing to the table.*] These are their cards.

JOHN.

[*Picking up the cards.*] "Mrs. Cloys," "Mr. Claude Aylmer Emptage," "Sir Fletcher Portwood." Mrs. Cloys—that's an aunt.

OLIVE.

[*Stonily.*]   An aunt——?

JOHN.

An aunt of Mrs. Fraser's.   What can they want with me ?

OLIVE.

Isn't it curious ! ·

JOHN.

I assure you I haven't the slightest idea.   I sup-pose nothing has happened to her !

OLIVE.

To Mrs. Fraser ?

JOHN.

Yes.

OLIVE.

Oh, no ; nothing ever happens to these women with fair and heavy eyelids.

JOHN.

[*Biting his lip.*]   Really ?

OLIVE.

You will see them, I suppose ?

JOHN.

I can't refuse to see them.

OLIVE.

May I—may I wait till they have gone ?

JOHN.

Oh, Olive——! [*She walks to the dining-room, he following her.*] I won't let them detain me very long.

OLIVE.

[*Rapidly, agitatedly, facing him, her hand on the door-handle.*] This is a most extraordinary visitation. These three people—her relatives—to come down on you like this, at such an hour !

JOHN.

I am sure you will find that their visit admits of a perfectly reasonable explanation.

OLIVE.

I've no doubt !

JOHN.

You shall have the fullest account of what passes between us.

OLIVE.

How shall I know it is a full account ?

JOHN.

[*Leaving her.*] Oh——!

OLIVE.

[*Advancing quickly.*] No, I don't mean that ! [*Her hand to her heart.*] Oh, do make some allowance for me, for my state of mind !

JOHN.

[*Turning abruptly.*] Have you the courage to meet these people with me ? If so, you can begin to-night to carry out your promise to serve Mrs. Fraser ; you can tell her relatives now what your intentions are towards her.

OLIVE.

[*Falteringly.*] Certainly, I have the· courage to meet them. [*Advancing tremblingly, breathlessly.*] But do you know where you are drifting, John ?

JOHN.

Where I am drifting——?

OLIVE.

Yes. I mean—what position are you willing to give me before these people ?

JOHN.

Position——?

OLIVE.

I couldn't submit to be treated as a culprit ; and there is only one other possible position for me.

JOHN.

What is that ?

OLIVE.

The—the—the wife.

JOHN.

[*Slowly.*] The wife.

OLIVE.

[*Tearfully.*] Oh——! oh, I would try !
    [*He leaves her, and walks about agitatedly.
    She sits on the settee, weeping.*

JOHN.

[*Rather wildly.*] Well, I—I only want to cleanse the slate. My cursed stupidity has smeared poor little Mrs. Fraser's character ; I want to put *that* right. It cuts me to the heart to see how wretched *you* are, Olive ; I want to put *that* right. Oh, if we fail again——!

OLIVE.

We c—c—can't fail again—it's impossible !

JOHN.

[*Desperately, throwing himself into the chair.*] All right ! Heaven have mercy upon us—we're reconciled ! Ring the bell. [*She rises and touches the bell-press, and with the aid of the mirror over the mantelpiece attempts to adjust her hair and straighten her bonnet, he watching her.*] By Jove, you have pluck !

OLIVE.

To face these people ?

JOHN.

[*With a short laugh.*] I call it true courage.

OLIVE.

It's nothing ; I am so happy. Oh, John, you shall never regret this.

QUAIFE *enters.*

JOHN.

[*Rising.*] Show Mrs. Cloys and the two gentlemen in here.

QUAIFE.

Yes, sir.

JOHN.

Tell them that Mr. and *Mrs.* Allingham are now disengaged.

QUAIFE.

Yes, sir. [*He withdraws.*

OLIVE.

[*Turning sharply.*] *Mrs.* Allingham—— ?

JOHN.

It wouldn't be quite fair to spring you upon them suddenly——

OLIVE.

You've given them warning; they may hurry away, to avoid me !

JOHN.

No, no——

OLIVE.

If they did do such a thing——! [*Agitatedly.*] Gur-r ah ! I can't get my bonnet to sit straight. May I take it off, and receive them as if I were— at home ?

JOHN.

If you would rather do so——

OLIVE.

[*Going to the dining-room door.*] Is there a mirror in here ?

JOHN.

Yes. [*She goes out hurriedly.*] Let me hold the lamp for you——

[*He follows her. After a brief pause. QUAIFE re-enters, showing in MRS. CLOYS, SIR FLETCHER PORTWOOD, and CLAUDE. QUAIFE withdraws.*

MRS. CLOYS.

[*After looking round the room.*] The wife.

SIR FLETCHER PORTWOOD.

The wife !

MRS. CLOYS.

Who could have anticipated anything so extraordinary !

SIR FLETCHER PORTWOOD.

[*Walking about uneasily.*] Harriet, your theories and suspicions have involved us in an entanglement of—ah—an unexpected kind.

CLAUDE.

[*Moodily.*] A reg'lar mess, I call it.

SIR FLETCHER PORTWOOD.

I wish your choice of expressions was a little happier, Claude——

MRS. CLOYS.

The boy is right ; and we must get out of this as quickly as possible.

SIR FLETCHER PORTWOOD.

Yes, yes ; yes, yes.

CLAUDE.

But I don't believe the woman will have the
daring effrontery to show her face to us ; to *me*
—the brother !

MRS. CLOYS.

If she does appear, Fletcher, how on earth are
we to explain our visit ?

SIR FLETCHER PORTWOOD.

Never explain, Harriet. I once explained in the
House——

MRS. CLOYS.

Devil take the House !

SIR FLETCHER PORTWOOD.

Harriet !

MRS. CLOYS.

Heaven forgive me !

SIR FLETCHER PORTWOOD.

You are unhinged—not yourself. No, no, we
must simply avail ourselves of any topic that presents itself.

MRS. CLOYS.

Mercy on us ! there's only one topic that *can*
present itself.

Sir Fletcher Portwood.

I am not often nonplussed. You had better watch me closely ; follow my lead—tsch !

John *enters with* Olive, *who is now without her outdoor apparel.*

John.

[*After bowing to* Mrs. Cloys.] How do you do, Sir Fletcher ? [*Nodding to* Claude.] How are you, Emptage ?

Sir Fletcher Portwood.

[*With a wave of the hand towards* Mrs. Cloys.] My sister, Mrs. Cloys.

John.

Mrs. Cloys, Sir Fletcher ; there have been some most unhappy differences between my wife and myself in the past, as you know too well. Unfortunately, she and I have not been the only sufferers from these differences ; we have dragged others along with us. However, we met this evening, half an hour ago, and are—reconciled——

Sir Fletcher Portwood.

[*In a murmur.*] Very proper—very sensible——

John.

And I have my wife's authority for saying that her feelings towards Mrs. Fraser are now considerably—in fact, entirely—— But she will speak for herself. [*Presenting* Olive, *awkwardly.*] Er—my wife.

OLIVE.

[*To* SIR FLETCHER *and* MRS. CLOYS, *graciously.*]
Pray sit down. [MRS. CLOYS *sits again.*] Sir
Fletcher, we knew each other years ago——

SIR FLETCHER PORTWOOD.

I am delighted to renew—[*pulling himself up
uneasily*]—that is, of course——
    [OLIVE *sits on the left and* SIR FLETCHER
    on the right of the table.

OLIVE.

[*Addressing* MRS. CLOYS.]   Mrs. Cloys, it is
only fair to you that I should say at once that I
don't expect Mrs. Fraser's relatives to treat me at
all tenderly over the painful proceedings which
terminated to-day. [MRS. CLOYS *bows stiffly;* SIR
FLETCHER *eyes her anxiously.*] So I beg that you
will speak before me entirely without reserve.
[*Looking at* JOHN.] It is my husband's wish that
you should do so.

JOHN.

Certainly.
    [MRS. CLOYS *and* SIR FLETCHER PORTWOOD
    *sit staring before them in a glassy
    way;* OLIVE *again glances at* JOHN,
    puzzled.

OLIVE.

[*A little impatiently.*]   Naturally, Mrs. Cloys, I
can't think that you have taken this inconvenient
journey to-night without some very special, some
very definite object.

Sir Fletcher Portwood.

Er—so far as I am concerned, the object of my visit is in a great part attained when I have given Mr. Allingham my assurance that only absolute proof of his unworthiness will ever induce me to withdraw my friendship from him. I am nothing if not a just man——

John.

Genuinely obliged to you, Sir Fletcher.

Sir Fletcher Portwood.

Oh, I am not ashamed of my simple faith in young English manhood and in the efficacy of a training at one of our most honoured public schools. True, I was never a public-school boy myself——

Claude.

[*Leaning on a chair near the window, with his back to those in the room.*] Ha!

> [*All turn their heads towards* Claude, *surprised.*

Sir Fletcher Portwood.

[*Rising, and going to* Claude.] No, but I am still capable of rejoicing when I see the traditions of popular British institutions worthily upheld. The world was my public school——

Olive.

[*Changing her position.*] Mrs. Cloys——

Sir Fletcher Portwood.

[*Eyeing* Olive, *and returning quickly.*] Er—is there a question more vital, more absorbing, than

this great vexed question of Education? Is there
a question which calls more imperatively upon the
attention of thinking men——?

OLIVE.

[*Turning to him with a forced smile.*] But, Sir
Fletcher, you surely haven't brought Mrs. Cloys
all the way to Epsom that she may hear you
discuss Education with my husband?

SIR FLETCHER PORTWOOD.

[*Disconcerted.*] No, no. Good! ha, ha! good!
Excellent! Er—— [*Suddenly.*] Now, this cottage
—I wonder whether I may ask how many rooms?

OLIVE.

How many rooms?

JOHN.

Twelve.

OLIVE.

[*Between her teeth.*] Twelve.

SIR FLETCHER PORTWOOD.

The reason I put the question is this : my dear
brother-in-law, the bishop——

MRS. CLOYS.

[*Under her breath.*] Eh?

SIR FLETCHER PORTWOOD.

[*Looking at* MRS. CLOYS *significantly.*] The
bishop often suffers from the effects of severe
intellectual strain, and it has more than once struck

me that for a few weeks in the year this peculiarly invigorating air—— [*Going to the dining-room door.*] The arrangements appear to be most convenient. May I?

JOHN.

The dining-room.

SIR FLETCHER PORTWOOD.

[*Opening the door and peeping into the room.*] Delightful! I can picture the bishop sitting there, my sister there, myself, perhaps, over there —delightful! [*Closing the door and moving away, pointing to the other door.*] The hall and the little card-room I have seen. [*Rapping the table.*] But the grand question is, Mrs. Allingham —would you let? That's the point, Allingham— would you feel inclined to let?

JOHN.

Oh, if his lordship did us the honour of expressing a wish——

SIR FLETCHER PORTWOOD.

That's extremely good-natured. [*Trying to catch* MRS. CLOYS' *eye.*] You hear, Harriet?

MRS. CLOYS.

[*With a gulp.*] Yes.

SIR FLETCHER PORTWOOD.

[*Pointing to the steps.*] And here!

OLIVE.

[*Struggling to suppress her anger.*] The library—the library.

Sir Fletcher Portwood.

Have I permission ?

Olive.

Oh, by all means.
> [Sir Fletcher *bustles up the steps and enters the library.*

Sir Fletcher Portwood.

[*Out of sight.*]   Cheerful—very cheerful.   A paucity of volumes ; but the bishop would bring his own books.

Olive.

[*Quickly.*]   Sir Fletcher, while you are there, do examine the little clock on the mantelpiece. The case is modern oriental.

Sir Fletcher Portwood.

[*Out of sight.*]   Ah, yes, yes.

Olive.

I gave it to Mr. Allingham some years ago. Count those curious stones round the dial.   [*To* Mrs. Cloys, *rapidly but forcibly, dropping her voice.*]   Mrs. Cloys, I confess I find it difficult to accept Sir Fletcher's suggestion that you are engaged at this time of night in hunting for fresh air for the bishop.   I——
> [*Upon* Sir Fletcher's *disappearance,* Claude *advances and stands waiting for an opportunity to speak.*

CLAUDE.

[*Breaking in in a hollow voice.*]   As Mrs.
Fraser's brother——
[*All turn their heads towards* CLAUDE *again.*

OLIVE.

[*With clenched hands.*]   Oh ! I am endeavour-
ing to speak to Mrs. Cloys——

CLAUDE.

Pardon me.   As Mrs. Fraser's brother, and as,
perhaps, the chief sufferer from the result of to-
day's proceedings——

SIR FLETCHER PORTWOOD.

[*Appearing suddenly on top of the steps, no
longer carrying his hat.*]   What's this ?   What's
this ?

CLAUDE.   .

I refuse to be silenced.   As Mrs. Fraser's
brother, I desire to say that I did not expect to be
received to-night by the lady who has done her
best—her utmost——

SIR FLETCHER PORTWOOD.

S-s-sh ! s-s-sh !

MRS. CLOYS.

Be quiet, Claude, please !

OLIVE.

[*Rising and going to* JOHN.]   John, really——

JOHN.

[*Hotly.*] Look here, Emptage, you're a boy—
at any rate, a very young man——!

CLAUDE.

I am a truly unfortunate young man. A blight
has been cast upon my name at the very outset of
my career——

JOHN.

[*Bluntly.*] What career?

CLAUDE.

Well, when I am turning various careers over in
my mind——

MRS. CLOYS.

Enough. Claude——!

SIR FLETCHER PORTWOOD.

[*Coming down the steps.*] Why, when I was
five years younger than he I had already applied
my lever to the mountain. I first saw light in
forty-four——

OLIVE.

[*To* JOHN.] Oh——!

SIR FLETCHER PORTWOOD.

Forty-four; an easily remembered date—two
fours. And what was I doing at his age?

OLIVE.

Mrs. Cloys——

MRS. CLOYS.

Go away, Claude!

CLAUDE.

[*Retiring.*] Ha, at least I have had the courage to speak out——!

> [*He throws himself into a chair at the back, and in course of time falls asleep. His head is seen to drop back upon his shoulder; an arm hangs over the side of the chair.*

OLIVE.

[*Advancing to the table, imperatively.*] Mrs. Cloys——

SIR FLETCHER PORTWOOD.

I——

MRS. CLOYS.

[*Firmly.*] Excuse me, Fletcher; I believe Mrs. Allingham is looking to me for some further explanation. [*Sitting.*] Mrs. Allingham, happening to become acquainted to-day, for the first time, with several features of this disagreeable business, I thought—it was a fancy of mine—that I should like to meet Mr. Allingham—to talk over—to——

OLIVE.

[*Sitting.*]   To talk over——?

SIR FLETCHER PORTWOOD.

To thresh it all out with John—with Allingham.

OLIVE.

[*Quickly.*]   It has not been sufficiently threshed out, then, in the Divorce Court?

MRS. CLOYS.

[*Hastily.*] Quite sufficiently. [*Eyeing* SIR FLETCHER *reprovingly.*] My brother doesn't interpret me correctly. Er—as I have told you, it is a fancy of mine—to meet Mr. Allingham.

OLIVE.

Just to make his acquaintance?

MRS. CLOYS.

[*Steadily.*] Just to make his acquaintance.

JOHN.

[*Uncomfortably.*] Very pleased—very gratified——

OLIVE.

[*With a hard smile.*] This is rather an odd hour for such a call.

MRS. CLOYS.

It would have been earlier but for a little difficulty in discovering Mr. Allingham's whereabouts.

SIR FLETCHER PORTWOOD.

[*Genially.*] When ladies have fancies they don't study the hour before indulging them.

OLIVE.

I am afraid it *is* so in your family, Sir Fletcher.
[MRS. CLOYS *makes a movement, but restrains herself.*

JOHN.

[*In a low voice.*]   Olive——!

SIR FLETCHER PORTWOOD.

Er—the fact is my sister shares with me the Lavater-like faculty for judging character at sight.

OLIVE.

Judging character by face, manner?

SIR FLETCHER PORTWOOD.

Yes. I possess it in a remarkable degree. I remember——

OLIVE.

[*To* MRS. CLOYS.] Oh, I see ! You are here to —to form an impression of Mr. Allingham ?

MRS. CLOYS.

Sir Fletcher a little exaggerates my powers ; but I may confess I am, like many people, very sensitive to receiving impressions through such mediums.

OLIVE.

I hope your impressions of my husband will be to his advantage.

MRS. CLOYS.

[*Looking at* JOHN.] I think I may say at once that they are not unfavourable.

OLIVE.

Because the necessity you find for estimating my husband's character shows—you know what it shows.

MRS. CLOYS.

Mrs. Allingham——?

OLIVE.

It shows, obviously, that if you are uncertain as to my husband's innocence, you must be equally doubtful of the innocence of your niece, Mrs. Fraser.

MRS. CLOYS.

[*Rising.*] I—I beg that you will not put such a construction on what I have said——

OLIVE.

[*Rising.*] What other construction——?

JOHN.

Olive, you are not keeping your promise——

OLIVE.

[*Passionately.*] I will keep my promise when I am treated openly and fairly. [*Walking away.*] I feel something is going on here that I don't understand, that I am not allowed to understand.

JOHN.

[*To* MRS. CLOYS *and* SIR FLETCHER.] I am extremely sorry. But my wife is very fatigued and unstrung to-night——

SIR FLETCHER PORTWOOD.

Quite so, quite so. We are most inconsiderate, Harriet. Come—come ; another time——

OLIVE.

[*Turning.*]   No, no !   Mrs. Cloys——

MRS. CLOYS.

[*Facing* OLIVE *firmly.*]   Mrs. Allingham, I think, when we look back upon this evening, that you and I will be able to congratulate ourselves upon a considerable exercise of politeness.   But there are signs that neither of us is equal to a pro- longed strain.

OLIVE.

I beg your pardon ; I will be patient.   You need have no misgivings on my account.

MRS. CLOYS.

[*Formidably.*]   Perhaps not ; but I am begin- ning to be acutely conscious of my own weakness. [*Looking round.*]   Fletcher——

OLIVE.

[*Angrily.*]   Oh, oh !
> [*She paces the room ;* JOHN *joins her and
> is seen expostulating.* MRS. CLOYS
> joins* SIR FLETCHER.

JOHN.

Olive, Olive, be reasonable !

OLIVE.

I will be, when you and your friends are honest with me.
> [*She leaves him, as* QUAIFE *enters with a
> note upon a salver.*

Sir Fletcher Portwood.

[*Looking at his watch.*] Oh, Allingham, the hotel people were to send a carriage up for us; perhaps you'll get your servant——

John.

Certainly. [*To* Quaife.] Quaife—what's that?

> [*Upon entering,* Quaife *has encountered* Mrs. Allingham; *her eyes fall upon the letter on the salver.*

Olive.

[*Under her breath, staring at the letter.*] Ah-h-h!

Quaife.

Ma'am?

Olive.

[*Drawing 'back and speaking to* Quaife.] Well, give it to Mr. Allingham.

Quaife.

A boy has brought this, sir—waiting for an answer.

> [John *is about to take the letter; when he sees the writing upon the envelope he hesitates for a moment and draws his hand back; then he picks up the letter deliberately.*

John.

[*To* Quaife, *calmly.*] Wait; I'll ring.

> [Quaife *retires.*

OLIVE.

[*Pointing to the letter.*]   Isn't that letter from Mrs. Fraser?

JOHN.

[*After opening the letter.*]   Yes.   [*He reads the letter to himself.*]   Poor little lady !   This is bad news.

SIR FLETCHER PORTWOOD.

[*Agitatedly.*]   Really, Mr. Allingham, really ?

JOHN.

Don't you know ?   She has left her husband.

SIR FLETCHER PORTWOOD.

Er—yes, sir, we do know it—certainly we know it.   I was almost the last person she spoke to before she quitted her mother's house.   She is deeply attached to me.   [*Buttoning his coat.*] Where is she ?   Where is she ?

JOHN.

I gather she is waiting not very far from this house——

OLIVE.

[*Breathlessly.*]   Waiting——

JOHN.

She—she wishes to see me.

OLIVE.

[*In a low voice.*]   Oh, yes.   [*Sitting, her hands tightly gripped together.*]   Oh, yes.

JOHN.

[*Going to her and handing her the letter.*] Read it, please, Olive.

OLIVE.

[*After a pause, holding the letter between her finger and thumb, reading.*] "Station Hotel, Epsom. My dear old Jack——" [*Hastily returning the letter to* JOHN, *with a shudder.*] Take it from me !

JOHN.

[*Reading aloud.*] "My dear old Jack," [*Looking round, simply.*] We have known each other many years. [*Reading.*] " Oh, I have had such a job to find you. I shall plant myself at some quiet spot near your cottage and get a messenger to bring this to you. The messenger will show you where I am, if you will only consent to see me for a few moments on—[*looking round*]— on a matter of business."

[MRS. CLOYS, *concealed from the others by* SIR FLETCHER, *sinks on to the settee.*

SIR FLETCHER PORTWOOD.

Ha, a matter of business ! Of course, a matter of business.

JOHN.

[*Resuming.*] " I have left my husband. He turned against me at the end and crushed my one hope of being able to whitewash myself." The cur ! [*Resuming.*] " Am off to Paris the first thing in the morning. Very likely this is the last chance you will ever have of a word with your poor little friend, Theo." [*To* Sir Fletcher.] Sir Fletcher, I congratulate you on finding your niece ; please tell her that it is impossible for me to grant her request.

Olive.

[*Calmly.*] Oh, but wait. [*Rising.*] Surely it would be rather uncivil to refuse what Mrs. Fraser asks.

Mrs. Cloys.

[*Rising.*] I can be trusted to explain——

Olive.

But she is apparently in need of some business service which my husband can render her.

Mrs. Cloys.

Now that she is again in the hands of her relatives there can be no necessity for troubling Mr. Allingham.

Sir Fletcher Portwood.

Not the slightest ; not the slightest.

Olive.

Perhaps not. But before such a very curt message is sent to Mrs. Fraser, will you do me the favour of letting me have two or three minutes' conversation with my husband alone ?

Mrs. Cloys.

I—I am anxious to go to my niece.

OLIVE.

Two minutes. Please, John.

[JOHN *goes to the dining-room door and*
opens it. After a moment's hesitation,
MRS. CLOYS *goes to the door.*

MRS. CLOYS.

[*Turning.*] I beg that I may not be detained
longer.

[*She passes out;* JOHN *follows her, leaving*
the door open.

SIR FLETCHER PORTWOOD.

[*Standing over* CLAUDE, *shaking him.*] Wake
up, sir! wake up!

CLAUDE.

[*Waking.*] What is it? Eh? [*Rising.*] Hullo,
uncle!

SIR FLETCHER PORTWOOD.

You've been sleeping, sir; your manners are
appalling.

CLAUDE.

[*Stupidly.*] Where's aunt?

SIR FLETCHER PORTWOOD.

[*Leading him towards the door.*] In the next
room. Come, sir! You are deficient in tact,
delicacy——

[JOHN *re-enters.* SIR FLETCHER *passes him*
and goes out.

CLAUDE.

[*As he passes* JOHN.]   The dining-room?

JOHN.

[*To* CLAUDE.]   I shan't keep you more than a minute or two.

CLAUDE.

[*In the doorway, turning to* JOHN.]   Allingham, of course you and I can never again be the same to each other as we have been in the past; but may I take the liberty of foraging for a piece of cake?

JOHN.

[*Laying a hand on his shoulder.*]   Certainly.

[CLAUDE *goes out;* JOHN *closes the door
        and turns to* OLIVE.

OLIVE.

[*Facing him.*]   Well?

JOHN.

[*Advancing to her.*]   Well?

OLIVE.

Oh, could anything be clearer? It's easy enough now to see through the twaddle these people have been talking! Mrs. Fraser runs away from her husband, who believes her guilty; her relatives go in pursuit; they look for her and find her—where?

JOHN.

Her relations chance to be here when Mrs. Fraser sends for me——

OLIVE.

[*Mockingly.*]   Yes !

JOHN.

[*Referring to the letter.*]   Desiring to see me "for a few moments, upon a matter of business." That is all that can be made of it.

. OLIVE.

A matter of business !

JOHN.

This letter is not quite ingenuous, you infer.

OLIVE.

You've caught the tone of the lawyers exactly.

JOHN.

[*Hotly.*]   "A matter of business" is a lie, you mean ?

OLIVE.

Her arrival to-night is a remarkable coincidence.

JOHN.

A perfectly natural one.

OLIVE.

Why are you so eager, then, to avoid granting her the interview she asks for ?

JOHN.

Eager——!

OLIVE.

You send word to her that it's impossible.

JOHN.

Don't you make it impossible?

OLIVE.

No, I do not; I do not. I want you to meet her to-night; you've heard me say I wish it.

JOHN.

You mean that?

OLIVE.

If ever I meant anything in my life.

JOHN.

[*Referring to the letter.*] "I shall plant myself at some quiet spot near your cottage——"

OLIVE.

Ah, no! never mind the quiet spot near the cottage. Why can't you have your business interview here?

JOHN.

Here?

OLIVE.

[*In a low voice, her head drooping.*] Where we are now, while I—[*glancing toward the library*]—while I take my place in there.

[*There is a pause; JOHN stands looking at her a moment silently.*

JOHN.

And this is how you propose to carry out your undertaking to make amends to Mrs. Fraser?

[*He turns away from her.*

OLIVE.

Everything is altered since—since——

JOHN.

Since we were reconciled ! reconciled !

OLIVE.

Since I promised to aid Mrs. Fraser. The arrival of these people—that letter—has undone everything. [*Throwing herself upon the settee despairingly.*] Oh, they knew well enough where their bird would fly to ! [*Burying her face in the pillows.*] Oh, John, you'll kill me !

JOHN.

Ha, and so you would like to try Mrs. Fraser twice in one day ! And there would be no mistake this time, no doubt whatever ! Innocent or Guilty—guilty for choice !

OLIVE.

No, no, innocent. But I want to be satisfied. Only satisfy me !

JOHN.

Satisfy you ! My Heavens !

OLIVE.

Satisfy me ! satisfy me !

JOHN.

And what a model judge of this lady you would make—of any woman you are jealous of ! How scrupulously fair ! how impartial ? how——

OLIVE.

I would be just, John ; I would be !

JOHN.

[*Savagely taking a cigarette from the box on the table and sticking it between his teeth.*] Women of your temperament detect a leer in the smile of a wax doll.

OLIVE.

I give you my word that I will make every allowance for you both, if you will let me hear you together. You *are* old friends—"chums" was her expression for it in the witness-box to-day—and you are Jack and Theo to each other, naturally ; I am prepared for all that kind of thing. She can kiss you good-bye when she parts from you—[*beating her brow*]—I can comprehend even *that.* Only—only let me be satisfied by her general tone and bearing, by that unmistakable ring in the voice, that she has never been the arrant little profligate I once thought her.

[JOHN *is now sitting staring at the carpet and chewing the end of his cigarette.*

JOHN.

Supposing I—consented, and you were—satisfied——?

OLIVE.

[*Rising and speaking earnestly and rapidly.*] We are in June ; I would have her to stay with me. My friends, her own friends, should see that we were close companions. She should go everywhere with me ; my arm should always be through hers. I would get a crowd together ; she should receive my guests with me. Oh, by Goodwood week her reputation should be as sound as any woman's in England ! Come ! think of the dreadful days and nights she's given me, whether she's good or bad ! Come ! wouldn't that be generous ?

JOHN.

[*In a low voice.*] Look here ! you would swear to me you'd never use against her anything that might arise during our meeting—I mean anything that your cursed jealousy could twist into harm !

OLIVE.

Solemnly. If she proclaimed herself openly in this room to be your—[*with a stamp of the foot he rises*]—she should go scot-free, for me. If she behaved as an innocent woman, she might walk over me in the future, trample on me ; I'd be a slave to her. Only satisfy me !

> [*He goes to the writing-table, and rapidly scribbles a note. She watches him with eager eyes. When he has finished writing, he takes an envelope, rises, comes to* OLIVE, *and holds the note up before her.*

JOHN.

"Come to the cottage.—J. A."

> [*She inclines her head. He touches the bellpress. Then he encloses the note in the envelope, which he fastens and hands to* OLIVE.

OLIVE.

Why ?

JOHN.

Take it. [*She takes it wonderingly.*] I have met your demands so far. Now, if you wish to do a womanly thing, you'll throw that on the fire. [QUAIFE *enters ;* OLIVE *stands staring before her. Speaking in measured tones, keeping his eyes on* OLIVE.] Quaife, the note which Mrs. Allingham will give you is for the messenger.

QUAIFE.

Yes, sir.

JOHN.

If a lady arrives, ask her to sit down in the card-room ; let me know when she comes. I am alone, should the lady make any inquiries.

QUAIFE.

Very good, sir.

JOHN.

Olive, Quaife is waiting for the note. [*There is a pause ; then* OLIVE *turns suddenly and hands* QUAIFE *the note. He goes out. There is another pause.*] And after this—after this !—you and I ! Upon what terms do you imagine you and I will be after this ?

OLIVE.

Oh, if she comes out of it well, I will be so good to her——

JOHN.

[*Contemptuously.*] Ah——!

OLIVE.

[*Clutching his arm.*] I will make you forgive me for it; I will make you ! [*He releases himself from her almost roughly, and moves away, turning his back upon her.*] Of course, you will not mention to Mrs. Fraser that you and I are in any way—in any way——?

JOHN.

Reconciled ! [*Sitting on the settee, laughing wildly.*] Ha, ha, ha——! [*Turning to her.*] Why not?

OLIVE.

Naturally, she wouldn't open her lips to you at all if you did.

JOHN.

[*Waving her away.*] Faugh !

OLIVE.

[*Her hand to her brow.*] You are—very—polite. [*She walks slowly and painfully towards the steps, pausing in her walk, and referring to her watch.*] John, when the talk between you and Mrs. Fraser has—gone far enough, I will strike ten on the bell of the little clock in here. You understand?

JOHN.

When you are satisfied !

OLIVE.

[*Beginning to ascend the steps with the aid of the balustrade.*] When I am satisfied.

JOHN.

Olive——! [*She stops.*] It's not too late now for us to think better of playing this infernally mean trick upon her.

OLIVE.

[*Steadily, in a low, hard voice.*] Why, nothing can arise, during this interview, injurious, in the mind of any fair person, to Mrs. Fraser's reputation?

JOHN.

[*Starting to his feet.*] Nothing! nothing!

OLIVE.

Then I am clearly serving Mrs. Fraser's interests by what I am doing.

> [*She disappears into the library. After a brief pause, JOHN hastily goes to the dining-room door, and opens it slightly.*]

JOHN.

Mrs. Cloys! Mrs. Cloys!

MRS. CLOYS.

[*From the dining-room.*] Yes.

JOHN.

Let me speak to you? [MRS. CLOYS *enters; he closes the door sharply, speaking hurriedly and excitedly.*] I—I have altered my mind about meeting Mrs. Fraser——

MRS. CLOYS.

Altered your mind——?

JOHN.

I have sent a note to her by her messenger asking her to see me here.

MRS. CLOYS.

Mr. Allingham, I protest against this as quite unnecessary.

. JOHN.

Pardon me. [*Producing* THEOPHILA'S *letter, and speaking disjointedly, uneasily.*] On—on consideration, it seems to me that—that—for everybody's sake, I have to satisfy my wife that Mrs. Fraser's presence is due solely to the most innocent causes.

MRS. CLOYS.

Mrs. Allingham has, I take it, arrived at certain conclusions as to the motive of my visit?

JOHN.

She has.

MRS. CLOYS.

And now, Theophila following upon our heels——?

JOHN.

It is a most unfortunate accident——

MRS. CLOYS.

[*Eyeing him penetratingly.*] Mr. Allingham, you have no doubt whatever of the absolute genuineness of my niece's excuse for calling upon you?

JOHN.

Oh, Mrs. Cloys——!

MRS. CLOYS.

[*Sitting.*] Yes, I admit that I came here to-night to ask you to pledge your word to us that Theo should run no further risk from her—her acquaintanceship with you ; to entreat you, if she should be so base, so abandoned——

JOHN.

You mean you thought it possible, probable, that this lady had run away from her husband and friends with the deliberate intention of joining me—me ! [MRS. CLOYS *covers her eyes with her handkerchief.*] Great Heaven, I suppose there *is* no living soul who will believe in an honest friendship between a young man and a young woman !

MRS. CLOYS.

There are certain rules for the conduct of friendship, Mr. Allingham——

JOHN.

[*Excitedly.*] Rules ! The world is getting choked with rules for the conduct of everything and everybody ! What's the matter with the world that a woman has to lose her character and paint her face before she is entitled to tell a man her troubles, and hear his in return, across a dying fire, by lamplight, when the streets are still and a

few words of sympathy and encouragement stir
one like a sudden peal of bells——?

[*He stands by the fire, bowing his head upon
the mantelpiece.*

MRS. CLOYS.

[*Looking at him, and speaking in a low voice.*]
Ah! a dying fire, the lamplight, the still
streets——! The world is what it is, Mr. Allingham.

JOHN.

Yes, and it is a d——able world !

QUAIFE *enters.*

QUAIFE.

The lady has arrived, sir.

[MRS. CLOYS *rises.*

JOHN.

[*To* QUAIFE.] When I ring, show her in here.

[QUAIFE *withdraws.*

MRS. CLOYS.

[*Agitatedly.*] Mr. Allingham, you will not let
Theo slip through my fingers ; you won't let her
escape me——? [*Looking at him.*] Oh, I will
trust you so far.

JOHN.

You may. I only ask you to allow me to have
my interview with Mrs. Fraser undisturbed.

MRS. CLOYS.

Ah, if you knew how I hate the idea of this meeting between you two! [*Turning sharply.*] I've a feeling that something evil is going to result from it——!

JOHN.

I can only repeat, you're wrong in what you think of me—[*turning away*]—wrong, every one of you.

MRS. CLOYS.

[*Coming to him, her manner gradually changing to harshness, almost to violence.*] Well, understand me, Mr. Allingham! I'm inclined to—to half-believe in you ; you've an honest face and air—not that those things count for much ; but understand me : if you bring, in any shape or form, further harm to her——!

JOHN.

[*Indignantly.*] What further harm can I bring to her? You find me here with my wife——!

MRS. CLOYS.

Sir, you had a wife round the corner when you were engaged in destroying my niece's reputation in Lennox Gardens! [*Recovering her composure.*] But enough of that. [*Calmly, amiably.*] We do understand one another, do we not?

JOHN.

[*Shortly.*] Oh, perfectly.

MRS. CLOYS.

That's right. [*Arranging her bonnet strings, which have become slightly disordered.*] Excuse me for breaking out in this fashion. [*She goes to the door, he following her. At the door she turns to him with grave dignity.*] I'm afraid I've impressed you as being rather a tigress.

> [*She goes out. He closes the door after her and stands staring at the ground for a moment; then he gently turns the key in the lock and carefully draws the portière across the door. He is about to put his finger upon the bell-press when he pauses.*

JOHN.

[*In a low voice.*] Olive. Olive. I have not yet rung the bell. Do you stop me? [*A pause.*] Won't you stop me?

> [*He waits; there is no answer; with an angry gesture he rings the bell. After a brief pause* QUAIFE *enters;* THEO-PHILA *follows. She is dressed as in the previous Act, but is now thickly veiled.* QUAIFE *gives a puzzled look round the room and withdraws.*

THEOPHILA.

Advancing and speaking in a weak, plaintive voice.] Oh, Jack——! [*They shake hands, but in a constrained, rather formal way.*] Of course, we could have had our talk very well in the lane; but it's kind and considerate of you to ask me in.

JOHN.

Oh, not in the least. [*Confusedly.*] I—er—I—
Do sit down.

> [*She looks at him, expecting him to find her
> a chair. In the end, after a little un-
> certainty, she seats herself on the right
> of the table. In the meantime he ascer-
> tains that the door by which Theophila
> has entered is closed.*

THEOPHILA.

[*Lifting her veil.*] I'm afraid you're a little
angry with me for hunting you up.

JOHN.

Angry? Why should I be angry?

THEOPHILA.

Well, I suppose it *is* another—what d'ye call
it?—injudicious act on my part. But it seemed to
me, if I thought about it at all, that we came so
badly out of it to-day, that nothing matters much
now. At any rate, *my* character's gone.

JOHN.

[*Advancing a step or two but avoiding her eye.*]
No, no——

THEOPHILA.

Oh, isn't it? And yours has gone too, Jack;
only a man gets on comfortably without one.
[*Facing him, her elbows on the table.*] Well,
what do you think of my news?

JOHN.

[*Looking at her, startled.*] By Jove, how dreadfully white you are!

THEOPHILA.

[*With a nod and a smile.*] The looks have gone with the character—[*putting her hands over her face*]—both departed finally.

JOHN.

[*Coming a little nearer to her.*] Er—when you've had a little rest you will see everything in a brighter light——

THEOPHILA.

I should have kept my appearance a good many years, being fair and small. [*Removing her hands—looking up at him.*] You used to tell me I should last pretty till I'm forty-five. Do you remember? [*His jaw drops a little, and he stares at her without replying.*] Do you remember?

JOHN.

[*Moving away.*] Oh—er—yes——

THEOPHILA.

Is there anything wrong with you, Jack?

JOHN.

Wrong—with me? No.
    [*She shifts to the other side of the table, to be nearer to him. He eyes her askance.*

THEOPHILA.

Why don't you tell me what you think of my news?

JOHN.

Your news?

THEOPHILA.

[*Impatiently.*] You've read my letter, Jack. I'm a—what am I?—a single woman again; a sort of widow.

JOHN.

You are acting too hastily; you're simply carried away by a rush of indignation. Perhaps matters can be arranged, patched up. You mustn't be allowed to——

THEOPHILA.

Arranged! patched up! You don't realise what you're proposing! You wouldn't make such a suggestion if you had been a fly on the wall this afternoon while Mr. Fraser and I were—having a little talk. [*Struggling to keep back her tears.*] Alec—my husband—he was very much in love with me at one time. I never doubted that he would stand by me through thick and thin. He has done so pretty well, up till to-day, up till the trial, and then, suddenly, he—he——

[*She produces her handkerchief, rises, then moves away abruptly, and stands with her back to* JOHN, *crying.*

JOHN.

[*Turning to the fire.*] Mr. Fraser was taken aback, flabbergasted, I expect, by the tone adopted by the judge to-day ; there's that poor excuse for him. But a little reflection will soon——

THEOPHILA.

[*Drying her eyes.*] Oh, don't prose, Jack ! [*Turning.*] On the whole, I think it's better that he and I have at last managed to find out where we are.

JOHN.

[*Turning to her.*] Where you are ?

THEOPHILA.

You know, there's always a moment in the lives of a man and woman who are tied to each other when the man has a chance of making the woman really, really, his own property. It's only a moment ; if he let's the chance slip, it's gone, it never comes back. I fancy my husband had *his* chance to-day. If he had just put his hand on my shoulder this afternoon and said, " You fool, you don't deserve it, for your stupidity, but I'll try to save you——"; if he had said something, anything, of that kind to me, I think I could have gone down on my knees to him and—— [*Coming to* JOHN *excitedly.*] But he stared at the carpet, and held on to his head, and moaned out that he must have time, time ! Time ! Oh, he was my one bit of rock ! [*Throwing herself into a chair on the right.*] If he'd only mercifully stuck to me for a few months—three months—two—for a month——"

JOHN.

[*Going to her slowly and deliberately and standing by her.*] Mrs. Fraser. [*She looks up at him surprised.*] Of course, whatever future is in store for you, nothing—no luck, no happy times—can ever pay you back for the distress of mind you've gone through.

THEOPHILA.

Nothing, Jack—Mr. Allingham. [*Her hand to her brow.*] Oh, nobody knows! Oh, Jack, some nights—some nights—I've said my prayers.

JOHN.

I've found myself doing that too—in hansoms, or walking along the street.

THEOPHILA.

Praying for *me?*

JOHN.

[*Nervously.*] Y-yes.

THEOPHILA.

Oh, don't make me cry again! Oh, my head! oh, don't let me cry any more——!

JOHN.

Hush, hush, hush! What I want to say is this. You knew young Goodhew?

THEOPHILA.

Charley Goodhew—the boy that cheated at baccarat?

JOHN.

He didn't ; he was innocent.

THEOPHILA.

I'm sure he was, poor fellow.

JOHN.

Well, he told me, one day in Brussels, that he managed to take all the sting out of his punishment by continually reminding himself that it was undeserved, that there wasn't a shadow of justification for it. I suppose it would be the same with a woman who—who gets into a scrape ; an innocent woman ?

THEOPHILA.

It's good, under such circumstances, if you can feel a bit of a martyr, you mean ?

JOHN.

That's it. So, in the future, you must never tire of reminding *yourself* of the utter harmlessness of those hours we used to spend together in Lennox Gardens.

THEOPHILA.

They were harmless enough, God knows.

JOHN.

[*Earnestly, eagerly.*] God knows.

THEOPHILA.

And they were awfully jolly, too.

JOHN.

[*Blankly, his voice dropping.*]   Jolly——?

THEOPHILA.

You know—cosy, comforting.

JOHN.

Yes, yes—comforting. It was the one thing that kept me together during those shocking Pont Street days of mine.

THEOPHILA.

Our friendship ?

JOHN.

Our friendship. When I was in the deepest misery, the thought would come to me : "Well, I shall see my little friend to-day or to-morrow." And then I'd go through our meeting as I supposed it would be—as it always was——

THEOPHILA.

" 'Ullo, Jack ! good morning—or good evening. Oh, my dear boy, you're in trouble again, I'm afraid ! "

JOHN.

" Dreadfully. I shall go mad, I believe—or drink."

THEOPHILA.

" Mad—drink ; not you. Sit down and tell me all about it."

JOHN,

And so on,

TheophiLA.

And so on.   I had my miseries too.

JOHN.

Yes, you had your miseries too.

TheophiLA.

And then you invariably came out with that one
piece of oracular advice of yours.

JOHN.

Ah, yes.   " Don't fret ; it'll be all the same a
hundred years hence."

TheophiLA.

Which you couldn't act upon yourself.   How
vexed it used to make me—and the ponderous way
you said it !

JOHN.

Well, it was a good, helpful friendship to me.

TheophiLA.

And to me.

JOHN.

[*Standing a little behind her ; speaking calmly,
but watching her eagerly.*]   Because, all the while,
there was never one single thought of anything
but friendship on either side.

TheophiLA.

Why, of course not, Jack.

JOHN.

You'd have detected it in me, if there had been ?

THEOPHILA.

Trust a woman for that.

JOHN.

And if you had for a moment fancied that I was losing sight of mere friendship——— ?

THEOPHILA.

You !

JOHN.

What would you have done ?

THEOPHILA.

Oh, one day, the usual headache ; not at home the next—the proper thing. But, Jack, dear, I never felt the slightest fear of *you*—and that's what makes an end like this so cruel, so intolerably cruel.

JOHN.

Never felt the slightest fear of me——— ?

THEOPHILA.

No, never ; oh, of course, a woman can tell. Somehow, I knew—I knew you *couldn't* be a blackguard.

JOHN.

[*About to seize her hand, but restraining himself.*] God bless you ! God bless you ! [*He walks away and pokes the fire vigorously, hitting the coal triumphantly.*] Ah, ha, ha! [*Turning to* THEOPHILA.] I beg your pardon; you're in the most uncomfortable chair in the room.

[*She rises and crosses the room.*

JOHN.

[*Arranging the pillows on the settee.*] You must be so weary, too. I'm confoundedly stupid and forgetful to-night.

THEOPHILA.

[*Sitting on the settee.*] Fancy! a fire in June!

JOHN.

[*Walking about elatedly, dividing his glances between* THEOPHILA *and the library.*] I love to see a fire.

THEOPHILA.

[*Suddenly.*] Of course. [*Dropping her voice.*] I remember. [*He stops, staring at her.*] Do you recollect? [*Steadily gazing into the fire.*] That night when we were sitting over the fire in that little room in Lennox Gardens——

JOHN.

[*Hastily.*] Oh, yes, yes——

THEOPHILA.

"I shall always burn a fire, Theo," you said, "to bring back these nights, these soothing, precious talks in the quiet hours. Wherever I may be, I shall only have to light my fire to hear

you and to see you—to see you sitting facing
me——"

JOHN.

Ah, that evening—yes, I was terribly—terribly
down that evening. [*Wiping his brow.*] By-the-
bye, we—we mustn't neglect the—the—the matter
of business—the little matter of business——

THEOPHILA.

[*Rousing herself.*] Matter of——?

JOHN.

The matter of business you mention in your
letter——

THEOPHILA.

[*Rising.*] Oh, yes. [*Sitting on the left of the
centre table.*] Jack, I—I do hope you won't hate
me for asking you. You see, if I went to anyone
else, I should run a chance of having all my arrangements upset. I—I want to borrow a little
money——

JOHN.

Ah, yes, certainly—anything—I shall be most
happy——

THEOPHILA.

This is exactly how I am placed. Mr. Fraser
wanted to hurry me off abroad—ah ! that's done
with. Instead of that, you see, I've taken my
travels and my future into my own hands. I've
telegraphed to Emily Graveney, who was at
Madame MacDonnell's with us girls in the Rue
D'Audiffret-Pasquier. Emily is teaching in Paris

now—I hardly know how she scrapes along; she'll be mad with delight to have my companionship. But till the lawyers settle my position precisely as regards Mr. Fraser, I'm practically broke, penniless. It's a little ready-money I want.

JOHN.

[*Who has seated himself at the right of the table, while* THEOPHILA *has been talking.*] You have only to tell me how much——

THEOPHILA.

Well, I think I could tide over with fifty pounds. I'm afraid you haven't got it in the house, though. I don't **want a cheque**.

JOHN.

[*Taking out his keys and going to a table.*] I believe I *can* just make it up—— [*He opens a drawer in the writing-table, finds some bank-notes, counts them, then empties his sovereign-purse and screws the gold up in the notes.*] Within a pound——

THEOPHILA.

That's of no consequence. [*Rising.*] I'm awfully obliged to you; I knew you would—I—I——
[*He returns to her and finds her clutching the table unsteadily.*

JOHN.

[*Placing the money on the table.*] What's the matter?

THEOPHILA.

Nothing. [*Sinking back into the chair, with closed eyes.*]   I shall be all right in a minute.

> [*He brings her a glass of water and places it to her lips.   She sips the water for a little while, then gives a sigh.*

JOHN.

Better?

THEOPHILA.

I think so.

JOHN.

When did you last eat? [*She shakes her head feebly.   He puts the glass of water aside and fetches the biscuits.*]   Get two or three of these down.   Come—try——!

THEOPHILA.

[*Taking a biscuit.*]   Thank you.

> [*He places the biscuits on the table by her side and goes back to the other table.*

JOHN.

A glass of this champagne would pull you together.

THEOPHILA.

[*Nibbling the biscuit, her eyes still closed.*] Would it? [*He brings the decanter of champagne and a small tumbler.   She, speaking faintly, and opening her eyes.*]   Oh, do let me off this, Jack.

JOHN.

[*Pouring out some champagne.*]   No, no; stick to it—do.

THEOPHILA.

[*Watching him.*] That looks nice. [*She puts the remains of her biscuit on the table and stretches out her hand for the wine. He gives it to her ; she drinks.*] Oh ! oh ! oh—h—h—h ! [*There is a pause ; then she shakes herself, looks up at him, and breaks into a low, childlike little laugh.*] Ha ! ha, ha, ha ! I'd nearly gone, hadn't I ? [*Empty-ing her glass.*] Oh ! oh ! . . . . Fetch yourself a glass, and we'll drink luck to each other. Then I really must be off. The porter said the trains run every—every what was it ? [*He brings a glass which she fills, speaking animatedly.*] A tumbler ! oh, fie ! [*Filling her own glass.*] Oh, mine's a tumbler too ! [*Nodding to him.*] Our-selves ! [*Touching his glass with hers.*] Our two poor unfortunate selves ? [*They drink.*] Ha ! I don't care ! do you ?

JOHN.

Care——?

THEOPHILA.

A hang. For anything ; for what the judge said ; for what people think. Puh. Here's to our friend, the judge——! [*Drinking, nearly empty-ing her glass.*] I hope his wife's a cat who leads him a—— [*Jumping up suddenly, her eyes dilat-ing, holding her glass high in the air.*] Happiness and prosperity to Mr. Fraser ! [*Loudly.*] Mr. Fraser !

JOHN.

S-s-sh ! oh, hush !

THEOPHILA.

Fraser of Locheen ! [*She goes to the fireplace and flings the contents of her glass into the grate.*] Ha ! well, that's throwing good stuff after poor, isn't it ? [*She places her glass on the table ; the cigarette box is open; she takes a cigarette.*] The old sort ?

JOHN.

[*Quickly.*]   No, no——

THEOPHILA.

[*Striking a match.*]   Only a whiff.   [*Lighting her cigarette.*]   Sure I'm not in the way, Jack, if I rest here a minute or two longer ?

JOHN.

[*With a glance at the library.*]   C—certainly not.

THEOPHILA.

[*Throwing herself upon the settee in a careless attitude, smoking.*]   Oh, thank God for this rest ! [*Looking round.*]   So this is the little place you used to tell me about——

JOHN.

[*Standing, watching her apprehensively.*] Um——

THEOPHILA.

Phew !   Your fire's all right to look at—— ! [*She removes her cape from her shoulders and flings it away from her ; he picks it up, and places it over the back of a chair.*]   Never mind that rag. Are you likely to be in Paris ?

JOHN.

I—I'm not fond of Paris.

THEOPHILA.

[*Jumping up, and speaking volubly, excitedly, boisterously.*] Suppose that wire don't find Emily, and she doesn't meet me at the Nord to-morrow night. Ugh! cheerful! She may be dead. No, no; not Emily. Poor old Emily! Be sure you look me up if you *should* pass through. Rue Poissonnière, 18. You're bound to be rambling soon. How lucky a man is! Does just as he chooses. Good chap, So-and-so—awfully rackety—but the world would be a doooed deal livelier if there were more like him! That's what they all say of a man! . . . phew! . . . [*As she rattles on, she takes off her bonnet and clears her hair from her brow.*] But a woman! Well, look at *me*. Not that anybody *will* look at me, in Paris or elsewhere. I used to know several smart people in Paris! Now! Oh, my stars, won't they stalk distant objects when they see me coming along! [*Angrily.*] Ah, a gay time I shall have of it, shut up with Emily Graveney, with her red nose, and her poor, narrow chest, and her perpetual sniffle! [*She flings away her cigarette. Her hair is disordered, her breath comes quickly, there is a wild look in her eyes. Her bonnet falls to the floor. He paces the room distractedly.*] By Jove, I won't have a dull time, though! I shall only hang out with Emily long enough just to turn round. Then I'll take a little *appartement* of my own. Uncle Fletcher will make me an allowance; I won't touch a penny—

of—puh—*his* money. I'll let the world see how
happy I am without the character I've been robbed
of ! Yes, robbed of ! [*Laughing noisily.*] Ha,
ha, ha ! [*Snapping her fingers.*] Pish ! I shall
burst out laughing in the face of the whole world,
Jack—put my tongue out at the world, your wife,
my husband ! After the solemn farce we've all
gone through. [*Between her teeth.*] Y—y—yes,
they shall have a pretty picture in their minds of
me, t'other side of the Channel, with my finger to
my nose like a cheeky urchin ! Oh, my Heavens,
how I hate 'em—hate 'em—hate 'em !

JOHN.

Mrs. Fraser——! Mrs. Fraser——!

THEOPHILA.

Oh, the devilish injustice of it ! To think that
we're still married, Jack—you and I ! Hah ! the
mockery ! To think that we wander about the
world still with our owner's marks branded upon
us ! Ha, ha ! I believe I've an " F " branded
upon my shoulder—burnt in ! [*Running to him.*]
Oh, I won't bear it ! I can't bear it !

JOHN.

Hush, hush !

THEOPHILA.

I shall go mad if I can't pay out that wife of
yours ! [*Shrilly.*] She's ruined me ! I will be
even with her !

JOHN.

Hush—— !

THEOPHILA.

And with *him !*—that fish !—that cold, flapping fish ! [*Clinging to him suddenly.*] Jack——! I wouldn't bore you ! I wouldn't bore you, Jack——!

JOHN.

Bore me !

THEOPHILA.

Ah-h-h-h ! take me away ! Let's you and I go together !

JOHN.

[*Putting his hand over her mouth.*] Ah, for God's sake——! [*The clock in the library is heard to strike.*] It's too late ! too late!

THEOPHILA.

[*Drawing back, looking into his face.* Too late——? [*There is a sharp knocking at the dining-room door.*] What's that ? [*The knocking is repeated.*] Who is it ?

JOHN.

Mrs. Cloys is here.

THEOPHILA.

[*Her hand to her brow.*] Mrs. Cloys—aunt——!

JOHN.

Mrs. Cloys, Sir Fletcher, and your brother were with me when your note arrived. They want to see you.

THEOPHILA.

See me—see me——

JOHN.

[*Gripping her wrist.*] Pull yourself together, Mrs. Fraser——

> [*The knocking is again heard.* JOHN *goes to the door.*

THEOPHILA.

[*In a whisper.*] Jack! [*He pauses; she seems dazed.*] They—they haven't heard—a word of—oh, of what I've said to you?

JOHN.

Heard——! N-no. Are you ready?

> [*He pulls aside the portière, unlocks the door, and opens it.* MRS. CLOYS *enters;* SIR FLETCHER *and* CLAUDE *appear in the doorway.*

MRS. CLOYS.

You have tried my patience long enough, Mr. Allingham.. [*She goes to* THEOPHILA; JOHN *walks away, and stands with his back to those in the room.*] Come! you have had ample time for your *business interview.* [*Staring at* THEOPHILA.] What's wrong with you?

THEOPHILA.

[*Sinking into a chair.*] N-nothing.

MRS. CLOYS.

Where's your cape—and your bonnet?

> [THEOPHILA *looks round vacantly.*

SIR FLETCHER PORTWOOD.

Cape? cape? Here's a cape.

> [*He hands the cape to* MRS. CLOYS; *she
> snatches it from him, and puts it round*
> THEOPHILA's *shoulders.* CLAUDE *picks
> up the bonnet and brings it to* MRS.
> CLOYS, *then goes to the upper door, and
> stands there waiting.*

MRS. CLOYS.

[*Raising* THEOPHILA.] You are not well;
you are ill. Fletcher——! [SIR FLETCHER *goes
up to the steps leading to the library.*] Where
are you going?

SIR FLETCHER PORTWOOD.

My hat—— *He pushes the portière aside, then
draws back.*] Mrs. Allingham——! [*Hesitatingly.*] Er—I believe I have left my hat here,
Mrs. Allingham. May I——?

> [*He enters the library.*

THEOPHILA.

Mrs. Allingham! Mrs.—Allingham——!

MRS. CLOYS.

Yes, yes.

> [SIR FLETCHER *comes out of the library,
> carrying his hat.*

THEOPHILA.

[*To* MRS. CLOYS.] Mrs. Allingham! his . . . wife!

MRS. CLOYS.

Mr. and Mrs. Allingham have arranged their differences. [*Looking from* THEOPHILA *to* JOHN.] Why, don't you know?

SIR FLETCHER PORTWOOD.

[*Coming down the steps.*] Haven't you seen Mrs. Allingham?

THEOPHILA.

Seen her——?

SIR FLETCHER PORTWOOD.

This evening—here——?

THEOPHILA.

Here!

SIR FLETCHER PORTWOOD.

Your interview with Mr. Allingham has taken place in this room?

THEOPHILA.

In this room? Yes——

MRS. CLOYS.

Come——

SIR FLETCHER PORTWOOD.

Wait, Harriet, please! Allingham—Mr. Allingham—pardon me for putting such a question:

surely you have not allowed—allowed—been a
party to——?

MRS. CLOYS.

Allowed—what?

SIR FLETCHER PORTWOOD.

[*Looking toward the library.*] Harriet, you can
hear most distinctly, in the library——

MRS. CLOYS.

Hear——!

SIR FLETCHER PORTWOOD.

Overhear—certainly, overhear——

MRS. CLOYS.

No, no! [*Going to* JOHN.] Preposterous!
[*After a pause.*] Mr. Allingham, why should Mrs.
Allingham—be there! [JOHN *is silent.*] What
has passed between you and——? Your wife has
not been—listening?

JOHN.

[*Desperately.*] Mrs. Fraser—has said—nothing
to me that a—a just woman can bring up against
her——

MRS. CLOYS.

Listening!

JOHN.

[*Almost inaudibly.*] Yes. [*Passionately.*] But

you don't know——!   [*Calling in a loud voice.*]
Olive!   Olive——!

> [OLIVE *comes out of the library, and stands
> at the top of the steps.*   THEOPHILA *re-
> gards her for a moment blankly, then
> goes to the balustrade and stares up at
> her.   After a brief pause* THEOPHILA
> *joins* MRS. CLOYS, *but seeing* JOHN, *she
> comes unsteadily towards him and looks
> him in the face.   Then, as she turns
> away to* MRS. CLOYS, *she utters a groan,
> and tumbles to the floor at* JOHN'S *feet.*

END OF ACT THE SECOND.

THE THIRD ACT.

The Scene is the same as in the previous Act, but a few articles of furniture are differently disposed about the room. There is no fire ; and flowers decorate the fireplace. The windows are open and the light is that of a fine afternoon in summer. FRASER *is seated upon the settee.* JOHN ALLINGHAM *appears in the garden, looks into the room, glares fiercely at* FRASER, *coughs significantly, and walks away. When* JOHN *has gone,* FRASER, *glancing at the window, rises, and, with an angry exclamation, crosses the room.* MRS. CLOYS *and* JUSTINA *enter ;* MRS. CLOYS *is dressed as in the previous Acts, but without her bonnet and mantle ;* JUSTINA *is in a bright morning-dress.*

MRS. CLOYS.

[*To* FRASER.] She insists upon rising ; she will see you in a few minutes.

FRASER.

Thank you.

MRS. CLOYS.

She is excessively weak and shattered ; you must remember that.

171

FRASER.

Yes, yes. I can never adequately express my gratitude——

MRS. CLOYS.

[*Sitting upon the settee.*]   Tsch !

JUSTINA.

Aunt has been up with her the whole night.

MRS. CLOYS.

Not alone.   Mrs. Allingham——.

FRASER.

Mrs. Allingham——?

MRS. CLOYS.

Mrs. Allingham begged to be allowed to keep me company.   There was a little scene between us—but the woman is, to some extent, human, I find.

FRASER.

Oh, I've no doubt that Mrs. Allingham is ashamed of herself——

MRS. CLOYS.

I hope we are all ashamed of ourselves.   In the end I was far from sorry to have her companionship.   Your poor wife didn't come out of her swoon till nearly one o'clock this morning.   Then Dr. Erskine went home and Mrs. Allingham and I took our places by the bedside—[*to* JUSTINA]— till you arrived at breakfast-time, Justina.

JUSTINA.

[*To* FRASER.] And I brought old Sarah, who used to maid us girls when Theo was at home; she's dressing her now.

FRASER.

Mrs. Cloys, pray help me with your advice.

MRS. CLOYS.

[*Bridling.*] Oh—h—h——!

FRASER.

No, no—about Mr. Allingham. Ha! of course if we were Frenchmen we should fight a duel——

JUSTINA.

Certainly, my dear Alec, and he would kill you.

FRASER.

Perhaps; that doesn't follow.

JUSTINA.

It doesn't follow, because it can't follow. But he *would* kill you and everybody would say of you, "Serve him right; another unsatisfactory husband disposed of!" And you would be buried, and my sister would be free and would go to Trouville in August in her weeds, and we should all have a splendid time generally.

FRASER.

[*Dryly.*] If we were French.

JUSTINA.

Yes. [*Going to the window.*]   Why aren't we French ?

MRS. CLOYS.

Justina—— !

FRASER.

[*Advancing to* MRS CLOYS, *hesitatingly, uncomfortably—lowering his voice.*]   I can't deny that I have behaved in a very poor fashion to Theophila——

JUSTINA.

[*Looking into the garden.*]   Deny it ! no !

FRASER.

[*Turning to* JUSTINA.]   Please—— !   [*To* MRS. CLOYS.]   But you, Mrs. Cloys, have just admitted to me that, up till last night, your feelings towards her were at least as unjust as my own.

MRS. CLOYS.

Ah, I hope your contrition, now that the facts are known to us, is as sincere and as deep as mine, Mr. Fraser.

JUSTINA.

Oh, how miserable he looks !

MRS. CLOYS.

Who ?

JUSTINA.

Jack Allingham.

[*She goes out and disappears.*

FRASER.

[*Walking about angrily.*] There he is again !

MRS. CLOYS.

He has every right to be here.

FRASER.

It's in curious taste.

MRS. CLOYS.

I don't see that. He feels called upon to remain here to protect his wife. He might say,
with equal reason——

FRASER.

Hardly. He can take *his* wife away, and protect her elsewhere. But I am helpless. You tell
me it is a question whether Theophila ought to be
moved to-day or not——

MRS. CLOYS.

[*Referring to her watch.*] Dr. Erskine will
decide very shortly.

FRASER.

So, for how long, in Heaven's name, am I to
endure Mr. Allingham ? The fellow puts himself
in my way. If I walk in the garden, he appears
indoors at a window, and coughs in a menacing
fashion. When I enter the house the proceedings
are but slightly varied—I am inside ; Allingham
and his cough outside.

MRS. CLOYS.

I find him a simple-minded, boyish young man.

FRASER.

[*Looking through the balustrade into the library.*]
Do you?

MRS. CLOYS.

After all, the conspiracy he assisted at—for
which I can never forgive him—was carried out,
on his part, in perfect good faith to Theophila.

FRASER.

His share in it is singularly discreditable.

MRS. CLOYS.

[*Rising.*] You and I must remember that it is
through this discreditable act that we are able to
do justice to your wife.

JUSTINA *re-enters at the window.*

MRS. CLOYS.

[*To* JUSTINA.] Is Mr. Allingham there?

JUSTINA.

Yes, aunt.

MRS. CLOYS.

[*To* FRASER.] I assume you are anxious to
avoid any open quarrel with Mr. Allingham?

FRASER.

I simply wish to get my sick wife away as
speedily and as peacefully as possible, and then to

forget this gentleman—and his cough. [MRS. CLOYS *goes out at the window and disappears.*] Justina, surely you—*you*—resent this new attitude of Mrs. Allingham's? For months and months she is your sister's bitter, determined enemy; then, suddenly, she is allowed to sit up all night, nursing her?

JUSTINA.

You wouldn't grudge the woman her little bit of practical repentance? If ever I go in for repentance, let nobody try to do me out of it!

FRASER.

[*Impatiently.*] Repentance——!

JUSTINA.

[*Sitting on the arm of a chair.*] Oh, Olive Allingham didn't have too gay a time of it last night, take my word for it. When Theo came to, aunt tells me, her poor, overwrought brain wandered for an hour or so; that wasn't over-pleasant for Mrs. A. Theo went through the whole business from beginning to end, breaking off occasionally to say her prayers—praying that the case might end in her favour, and that the season's invitations would flow in as usual. Some-times she'd stop in the middle of it, and call out that she couldn't pray well while that creature was in the next room listening. Luckily she fell into a heavy sleep at about half-past two, and didn't wake till just as I turned up in response to aunt's telegram. But what a bad hour or two it must have been for Mrs. A. Picture it! The half-darkened room ; my little sister tossing about the bed, raving ; aunt sitting grimly on one side, with a handkerchief round her head ; and on the other side, hidden behind the bed-curtains, hardly daring to breathe, that woman, with her white face and her eyes almost out of their sockets !

SIR FLETCHER *enters, carrying some slips of paper covered with writing.*

SIR FLETCHER PORTWOOD.

Allingham has had really a most admirable cold luncheon laid in the dining-room. [*To* FRASER.] You haven't seen the dining-room ?

FRASER.

[*Shortly.*] No.

SIR FLETCHER PORTWOOD.

Really a capital lunch. Evidently it is intended that one should wander in and eat a wing of a chicken when one feels inclined.

JUSTINA.

You have been wandering, uncle, apparently.

SIR FLETCHER PORTWOOD.

A glass of sherry, merely. No—it is strange and unreasonable that it should be so, but it *is* so.

JUSTINA.

What is so ?

SIR FLETCHER PORTWOOD.

Why, one has rather a feeling of constraint in

sitting down to Allingham's table—at any rate until matters are in a more settled state. [*To* Fraser.] *You* wouldn't care to—to make the plunge?

FRASER.

Plunge—— ?

SIR FLETCHER PORTWOOD.

To break the ice?

FRASER.

Eat his lunch !

SIR FLETCHER PORTWOOD.

[*Sitting on the settee and arranging his papers.*] No, no ; I can quite understand——

JUSTINA.

[*Throwing her head back.*] Ha !

FRASER.

[*To her, angrily.*] I believe you would grin by the side of a grave.

JUSTINA.

[*Shrugging her shoulders.*] *Cela dépend.*

FRASER.

[*Turning away in disgust.*] Ah !

JUSTINA.

[*Jumping up.*] Oh, I've had my bad days lately—plenty of 'em ! This morning the atmosphere's a bit clearer. [*Gaily.*] Tra, la, la !

FRASER.

The woman who can laugh under such circumstances——

JUSTINA.

[*Turning upon him.*] Laugh ! My dear Alec,
if you had learnt to laugh when you acquired
your other accomplishments, you would have been
able perhaps to keep my sister out of the Divorce
Court.   [*She goes out.*

SIR FLETCHER PORTWOOD.

[*Fussing with his papers.*] Fraser—— [FRASER
comes to him.] When I got to my hotel here
last night I jotted down the—the—the leading
points—the leading features——

FRASER.

Leading features——?

SIR FLETCHER PORTWOOD.

Of this awkward affair between you and the
Allinghams——

FRASER.

[*Impatiently.*] There is now no question
between me and the Allinghams——

SIR FLETCHER PORTWOOD.

[*Rising.*] My dear Locheen ! A lady deliberately stations herself in that room, with the cogniz-
ance and approval of her husband, to listen to——

Fraser.

I wish to forget all that occurred last night. It is done with.

Sir Fletcher Portwood.

Pardon me ; it cannot be done with ; it ought not to be done with, without the most complete apology—I will not, for reasons you will presently appreciate, hint from which side. [*Going to* Fraser, *buttonholing him.*] Do you know what has suggested itself to me, Fraser?

Fraser.

[*Releasing himself.*] No.

Sir Fletcher Portwood.

Why, sir, if ever there was a matter for reference, for arbitration, this is one !

Fraser.

[*Between his teeth.*] Arbitration——?

Sir Fletcher Portwood.

Good Heavens, when I open my *Times* in the morning, and glance at the law reports, how often have I occasion to remark, " *That* scandal might have been averted, and *that*, and *that*——" if only the intervention of some cool, level-headed person had been secured, the intervention of some one possessing the rarest of all gifts—the judicial faculty !

FRASER.

The gift is rare enough upon the bench.   People
shrink from having their concerns adjudicated by
a meddlesome amateur.

SIR FLETCHER PORTWOOD.

I sent Claude to town for his mother at ten
o'clock this morning.   When *they* arrive, the
family will be complete—with the exception of
my brother, Thomas Osborne Portwood, who is in
Australia ; a deplorable case.   [*Looking about
him.*]   Arbitration dispenses with legal parapher-
nalia.   A table, writing materials, a few chairs
arranged—[*his eye falling upon a table*]—a table.
[*He moves the table and stands, disposing, by gesture, of an imaginary audience.*]   Seated here, I
should command the room.   [*Pushing the settee
a little farther towards the left.*]   This thing
must be differently placed.   Chairs there—and
there——   [*To* FRASER.]   Locheen, would this
be the better room, I wonder, or the library ?

FRASER.

[*Who has lapsed into thought, rousing himself.*]
Eh, for what ?

SIR FLETCHER PORTWOOD.

For the arbitration ?   [FRASER *impatiently starts
to his feet as* MRS. CLOYS *enters at the window with*
JOHN.]   Oh, Mr. Allingham, if you will give me
just a moment or two——

Mrs. Cloys.

[*Taking* Sir Fletcher's *arm and drawing him aside.*] Not now, Fletcher.

Sir Fletcher Portwood.

[*Annoyed.*] Harriet——!

[Sir Fletcher *and* Mrs. Cloys *stand outside the window, talking.* John *comes and faces* Fraser.

John.

[*With an effort.*] I am sorry to hear, Mr. Fraser, that you have been annoyed, while a visitor at my house, by the persistency of my cough.

Fraser.

If I could have assured myself, Mr. Allingham, that your cough was a genuine one, it would not, however violent and grave its attacks, have occasioned me the smallest concern.

John.

I admit the cough was not genuine. I employed it as a sign that I was at hand should you wish to have an explanation with me.

Fraser.

The invitation might have been more explicitly phrased.

John.

It was clear enough for most men. At any rate, I hope the invitation is sufficiently plain now.

FRASER.

Quite.

JOHN.

You decline it, or accept it?

FRASER.

If I hesitate, it is because I hardly know in what language you would choose for me to reply.

JOHN.

Language——?

FRASER.

Words—or a cough?

JOHN.

Oh, whichever you find most procrastinating and evasive.

FRASER.

[*Coolly.*] I decline your invitation, Mr. Allingham ; I have nothing to say to you.

JOHN.

[*With clenched hands.*] Nothing!

FRASER.

Nothing.

JOHN.

[*Glances at* MRS. CLOYS, *then advances closely to* FRASER *and speaks to him in a low voice, beside himself with anger, but betraying nothing by gesture.*] Fraser, *you* are actually responsible for the occurrences of last night. You have never

understood your unfortunate wife; but yesterday
your behaviour to her was cruel, brutal. I charge
you with acting to her like a brute.

FRASER.

[*Looking at him immovably.*] Well?

JOHN.

Well——!

FRASER.

I repeat, I have nothing to say to you, Mr.
Allingham.

> [*After a pause,* JOHN *retreats from* FRASER
> *and sits upon the settee, leaning his
> head upon his hands and uttering a
> groan.*

JOHN.

Fraser, I promised Mrs. Cloys, out in the
garden just now, that I would make an attempt to
soften matters between us, and—and—offer you
some civility—and so on. I began fairly well—
[FRASER *bows*]—and then the conversation took
another line. However—[*rising, speaking with
an effort, not looking at* FRASER]—let me say
that my house is quite at Mrs. Fraser's disposal—
[*with a gulp*]—and at yours for as long as she
honours me—as you both honour me—by remain-
ing here. [FRASER *again bows,* JOHN *glares at
him.*] As for ourselves, whenever we encounter
each other, I will be careful to look in an opposite
direction. Perhaps you will be good enough to
follow the same course.

FRASER.

It is one that would have suggested itself to me.

JUSTINA *enters.*

JUSTINA.

Alec, Theo is coming in to see you.

[JOHN *goes out quickly ;* JUSTINA *speaks to* MRS. CLOYS.

MRS. CLOYS.

[*Entering the room and addressing* FRASER.] Theo is ready.

[MRS. CLOYS *goes out as* SIR FLETCHER *enters the room.*

JUSTINA.

[*To him, significantly.*] *Now,* perhaps a little lunch, Uncle Fletcher——

[*She goes out by the dining-room door.*

SIR FLETCHER PORTWOOD.

[*To* FRASER.] Of course, my sister Harriet throws cold water upon my proposal——

FRASER.

Proposal—— ?

SIR FLETCHER PORTWOOD.

Arbitration. [FRASER *walks away and eyes the upper door anxiously and expectantly.*] But when did Harriet fail to throw cold water ! I shall sound Allingham and get his views. After all, Harriet is not essential ; Harriet is not——

> [*While speaking he goes to the table, takes up the inkstand and blotting-book and carries them to the other table.*

FRASER.

[*To* SIR FLETCHER.] Sir Fletcher, Theophila understands that she is to see me here alone——

SIR FLETCHER PORTWOOD.

[*Abstractedly.*] I am off, I am off. [*Stopping at the door, looking at the table and slowly tapping his forehead.*] Pens—paper ; two p's.

> [*He goes out.* FRASER *comes to the dining-room door, and carefully draws the portière ; then he walks away as* MRS. CLOYS *enters by the upper door with* THEOPHILA *leaning upon her arm.* THEOPHILA *is dressed as in the preceding Acts, but without bonnet or cape.* MRS. CLOYS *places* THEOPHILA *upon the settee, then goes out at the window, and disappears.* FRASER *takes a chair and sits.*

FRASER.

You—you are very ill, Theophila?

THEOPHILA.

[*In a low, level, weary voice, her eyes turned from him.*] No ; I have just escaped being ill, they say.

FRASER.

I have been out all night, taking steps to find
you ; your aunt's telegram did not reach me till
late this morning.   I hurried here directly.

THEOPHILA.

[*Indifferently, her thoughts elsewhere.*]   Oh ?

FRASER.

I hope they told you so.

THEOPHILA.

Yes—I think they did. [*Rousing herself
slightly.*] When did you receive the news that
I'd—I'd——?

FRASER.

That you had——?

THEOPHILA.

Run away ?

FRASER.

Justina came to Lennox Gardens last night at
about half-past six.

THEOPHILA.

It hadn't struck you as at all likely——?

FRASER.

No.

THEOPHILA.

Men *don't* think on some points, I suppose.
They hit ; they never expect to see a bruise.

FRASER.

The two days we passed in court, Theophila, set
me quite beside myself. I am here to express my
deep, my unfeigned regret for my treatment of you.
I—I humbly beg your pardon.

THEOPHILA.

[*Looking at him for the first time, in an expres-
sionless way.*] You know what happened last
night?

FRASER.

[*With assumed indifference.*] Mrs. Cloys—told
me—[*with a wave of the hand*]—oh, yes.

THEOPHILA.

I asked her to tell you all. She has told you *all?*

FRASER.

[*Nodding agitatedly.*] For God's sake, let us
never again refer to the subject. Forget my share
of yesterday and I will forget yours. [*Moving his
chair to the head of the settee, to be nearer to her.*]
Theophila, everything you planned that we should
do to reinstate you shall be done ; I am prepared
to go in with your schemes, heart and soul ; all
your suggestions shall be acted upon promptly.

THEOPHILA.

[*Moving away from him ; then, after a brief
pause.*] No, thank you, Alec.

FRASER.

[*Staring at her.*] No——?

THEOPHILA.

I'd rather not, now.

FRASER.

Why not?

THEOPHILA.

Things are different.

FRASER.

In what way?

THEOPHILA.

I feel very different. When I asked you yesterday afternoon to lend me a helping hand I was asking for my right. It's true we haven't got on well together; you've been in one place, I in another, for more than half our married life. It's true I've been miserable and lonely, and have told my tale often enough to him—Mr. Allingham——

FRASER.

[*Between his teeth.*] Yes, yes.

THEOPHILA.

But, throughout everything, I've never been disloyal to you; I've always been fair to you when speaking of you behind your back; though I've hated you sometimes, I wouldn't have let a living soul say a word against you in my presence. This is truth! truth! Oh, I know I've been vilely brought up! 'Tina and I are vulgar and slangy, and generally bad form; and we were once what's called "fast," I suppose. But our fastness didn't

amount to much; it was only flirting, and gig-
gling, and dodging mother, and getting lost in
conservatories and gardens. Oh, what fools girls
are! No, till yesterday I've been only silly—
silly—nothing but silly—till last night——! till
last night——!

FRASER.

[*Rising and pacing the room.*] You were no
more yourself last night than I was *myself* yesterday afternoon!

THEOPHILA.

[*Sitting upright.* Who says I was not myself?
It *was* myself, the dregs of myself, that came to
the top last night!

FRASER.

The—the—circumstances—under which you—
you behaved as you did——

THEOPHILA.

[*Hiding her face in the pillows.*] Oh, don't
remind me of it!

FRASER.

I mean, you were weak—ill——

THEOPHILA.

You mean nothing of the sort . . . oh-h-h-h,
how horrid I must have looked . . . .!

FRASER.

They were mere words you were speaking——

THEOPHILA.

It was *me—me!*

FRASER.

Surely, if I see no reason why you should not claim my help——?

THEOPHILA.

I see a reason—that's enough. I repeat, what I asked of you yesterday was my right, my right. But to-day—to-day it would be accepting a favour from you——

FRASER.

Favour !

THEOPHILA.

Favour. A poor, tawdry little thing I've always been ; but I've been proud—yes, very proud —like every woman who is square and honest. But now——! No, if I could pull myself up again, I'd do it, for mother's sake and 'Tina's ; but never, never, never, after last night, could I accept a favour from my husband !

FRASER.

I hear from your aunt that Mrs. Allingham— this man Allingham's wife!—generously offers to take you under her wing. Is it so ?

THEOPHILA.

[*Leaning back, her eyes closed.*] Aunt brought me a message to that effect from Mrs. Allingham this morning.

FRASER.

What answer did you send?

THEOPHILA.

None; I am going to see Mrs. Allingham.

FRASER.

I think I understand.

THEOPHILA.

Understand?

FRASER.

This lady's proposal is, after all, one worth con-
sidering. It would be a double triumph for you
to ride back into the shabby little circle you regard
as " society " in her coach. It would be a triumph
over *me* in the first place—over *me!*

THEOPHILA.

[*Opening her eyes and speaking calmly in a
subdued voice.*] Alec—[*glancing over her shoulder*]
is aunt out there?

[*He goes to the window and looks out.*

FRASER.

Yes.

THEOPHILA.

Call her, please.

[*He disappears. She rises feebly, and, with
an effort, pushes away the chair* FRASER
*has placed at the head of the settee; then
she sinks into it.* MRS. CLOYS *enters at
the window with* FRASER, *and comes to*
THEOPHILA.

MRS. CLOYS.

My dear—— ?

THEOPHILA.

Will you ask Mrs. Allingham to be good enough
to come to me?

MRS. CLOYS.

You are equal to seeing her?

THEOPHILA.

Yes—at once.

MRS. CLOYS.

Why are you sitting here?

THEOPHILA.

[*Irritably.*] Oh, I am not going to appear
quite a wreck before Mrs. Allingham. Find her,
aunt.

[MRS. CLOYS *goes out.* FRASER *brings a
footstool to* THEOPHILA *and places it
under her feet. She nods in acknowl-
edgement.*

FRASER.

[*Sarcastically.*] You must not forget to thank
Mrs. Allingham for taking her place by your bedside all last night.

THEOPHILA.

[*Indignantly.*] Ah, it was shameful of aunt to
have allowed that! She hid herself behind the
curtains and peeped at me. She saw how ugly I
was! I'll never forgive aunt for permitting it!
Oh——!

FRASER.

[*Glancing at the door.*] S-s-sh—— !

[*He walks away as* OLIVE *enters, followed
by* MRS. CLOYS. OLIVE *is dressed as in
the previous Act. Upon encountering*
FRASER *she slightly inclines her head
to him, with eyes averted ; he bows stiffly
She then comes and stands before*
THEOPHILA.

OLIVE.

[*To* THEOPHILA.] I—I hope you are better,
Mrs. Fraser.

THEOPHILA.

Thank you, yes. [*Turning her head.*] Don't
go yet, aunt—nor you, Alec. [*To* OLIVE.] Mrs.
Allingham, my husband comes to me to-day asking
me to go back home with him, in order that, after
all, we may commence together to fight the
" shabby little circle " to which I have, I dare say,
attached a great deal too much importance.
Well, I've declined to go back—declined. But
Mr. Fraser has an idea that I'm treating him
spitefully because I've found a powerful friend in
you.

OLIVE.

Mrs. Fraser, I—I do beg of you not to act
hastily, and without good advice. Of course, you
are angry, justifiably angry——

THEOPHILA.

Ah—— !

OLIVE.

But pray take time to reflect. Oh, I entreat you
to try—in a little while, when you feel less bitter—
to try to see your way clear to—to——

THEOPHILA.

To do what?

OLIVE.

To accept both Mr. Fraser's help—and mine.

[THEOPHILA *partly rises, as if about to make
some indignant response, but restrains
herself.*

THEOPHILA.

I—I can only make the same reply to you, Mrs.
Allingham, as I have just made to my husband—
thank you, no.

OLIVE.

You cannot right yourself in the eyes of people
without Mr. Fraser's assistance or mine. And
especially mine! You couldn't accomplish it
thoroughly with *his* help alone; it would be
impossible.

THEOPHILA.

Very well then, it's impossible.

OLIVE.

[*To* FRASER.] Mr. Fraser—— [FRASER *advances a few steps.*] Perhaps, by and by, you
will add your persuasions to mine that your wife
will accept me as your ally?

FRASER.

[*Stiffly.*] Mrs. Allingham, I regret that what you suggest is, so far as I am concerned, quite out of the question.

OLIVE.

Mrs. Cloys—[FRASER *retires as* MRS. CLOYS *approaches*]—I am sure *you* can understand the value of the services I am able to render your niece.

MRS. CLOYS.

Oh, perfectly.

OLIVE.

Then you will try to induce her——?

MRS. CLOYS.

Ah ! you must excuse me, Mrs. Allingham——

OLIVE.

You will not ?

MRS. CLOYS.

I may tell you that I anticipated her rejection of your proposal directly you communicated it to me——

OLIVE.

Indeed ?

MRS. CLOYS.

And I must say—[*looking at* THEOPHILA]—that I fully sympathise with the—ah—the feelings of——

OLIVE.

[*Rigidly.*] Of Mrs. Fraser ?

MRS. CLOYS.

[*Politely.*] Of Mrs. Fraser. [QUAIFE *enters, and advances a few steps towards* MRS. CLOYS, *who speaks to him quickly.*] Has——?
> [*She breaks off, looking at him significantly.*

QUAIFE.

Yes, ma'am.

MRS. CLOYS.

[*To* FRASER.] Mr. Fraser, may I trouble you to follow me? I have something to say to you. [QUAIFE *withdraws. To* THEOPHILA.] I must run away for a few. moments. Shall I send Justina to you?

OLIVE.

[*Quickly.*] Oh, Mrs. Fraser, let me speak a few words to you while no one is present——!

THEOPHILA.

Certainly.
> [MRS. CLOYS *passes her hand over* THE-
> OPHILA's *head caressingly, then hurries
> to the door.*

MRS. CLOYS.

Mr. Fraser——
> [*She goes out,* FRASER *accompanying her.*
> OLIVE *looks round the room, then sits,
> slowly and deliberately, upon the settee.*

OLIVE.

[*After a little pause.*] Forgive me.

Theophila.

Forgive you—— !

Olive.

Oh, do make the effort !

Theophila.

I can't understand your asking for my forgiveness, wanting it.

Olive.

Endeavour to understand me. I don't remember that it ever struck me, when you and I were—
friends, that your disposition was a jealous one.

Theophila.

No ?

Olive.

It isn't, is it ?

Theophila.

I couldn't go the lengths you've gone, from
jealousy, if you mean that.

Olive.

[*Sadly.*] Ah——!

Theophila.

Oh, don't you think that enough has been done
in the name of jealousy ? For months and months
it has made a hell of my life, your jealousy.
People have seen me walking about looking merry ;
but what sort of days and nights does a woman
really spend with the Divorce Court looming before

her? "Allingham *versus* Allingham, Fraser inter-
vening!" that's the air you've kept me dancing to
since—goodness knows when the music first struck
up! And now I'm to forgive you, offhand, because—you happen to have a jealous disposition'!

OLIVE.

[*Falteringly.*] You were sustained all the time
by the knowledge that you were an innocent, per-
secuted woman——

THEOPHILA.

Much good did my innocence do me yesterday
when they gave me "the benefit of the doubt," and
sent me out of the court ruined!

OLIVE.

It does you this much good—that now *I* am
satisfied as to your innocence I am prepared to
serve you humbly and faithfully. Oh, Mrs. Fraser,
I would be a true friend to you this time! [*Rising
and standing before* THEOPHILA.] Come, forgive
me!

THEOPHILA.

[*In a low voice.*] Well, for the months of awful
trouble you gave me, and for those two days in
the Divorce Court—yes, you're welcome to my
forgiveness for all that. [*Her voice hardening,
her hands clenched.*] But not for last night!

OLIVE.

You mustn't make me wholly responsible for
what took place last night.

THEOPHILA.

I do hold you responsible. Why—they've told me the story—I know that, when my note to your husband was handed to him, he wanted to send a message to me excusing himself from meeting me. Did you let the message go? There was I waiting out in the lane, my people in this room, all in a fidget to hurry to me and take me away. Did you let them come to me? No, you huddled them out of the way, and then drew your husband into your plot, and trapped me in here. I was the poor rat, half dead, who had been well worried, but who'd a little life still left ; so you had me in, panting, and got another few minutes' sport out of me——

OLIVE.

[*Her hands to her brows.*] Oh, don't, don't ! Mrs. Fraser, at any rate, it was through last night that you cleared yourself——

THEOPHILA.

[*Rising, and speaking fiercely.*] Cleared my-self ! Yes, and a pretty price you were the cause of my paying for " clearing myself " ! Do you think I'd have willingly cleared myself at that cost ? Ah, no decent woman could afford it ! Cleared myself !

OLIVE.

You were mad when you—— You were mad.

THEOPHILA.

You know better ! I was sane enough ! But mad, or sane, or—or whatever I was, I shall never think the same of myself again, never feel quite the same again. And to-day I'm to forgive you for it! No, if you came to me and told me that you'd just saved the life of some one dear to me, I couldn't forgive you for last night. I couldn't! No woman could.

> [OLIVE *walks away and stands, looking out into the garden.*

OLIVE.

[*After a pause, speaking in a hard voice.*] Excuse me for saying so, Mrs. Fraser, but I think you regard your share in the affair of last night more as a schoolgirl would regard it, than as a woman; rather sentimentally, in fact.

THEOPHILA.

Thank God, I'm able to do *that!* Sentimentally? Well, ninety-nine women out of a hundred are kept fresh and sweet by nothing better than mere sentiment. [*Sitting upon the settee, a little faintly.*] Where's 'Tina?

> [OLIVE *turns and comes to her; she is wiping the tears from her eyes.*

OLIVE.

You know, if you wished to have your revenge on me, you have it.

THEOPHILA.

Revenge? I?

OLIVE.

[*Turning from* THEOPHILA, *her hand playing with the arm of the chair.*] The services I thought

you would allow me to render you are the only
means by which I could hope to get my husband
to overlook my behaviour of last night.   He won't
speak to me to-day.

THEOPHILA.

I'm sorry.

OLIVE.

After what. has happened my one hold on him
is through the reparation I could make you.   And
now—and now—you——   [*Throwing herself into
the chair, crying.*]   Oh, it's like begging to you !

THEOPHILA.

Nothwithstanding — all you've done — you're
anxious to make it up with your husband, aren't
you ?

OLIVE.

[*In a whisper.*]   You needn't ask ; you've
heard all about it.

THEOPHILA.

Do you think that, with your nature, you could
ever be happy with him, and make him happy?

OLIVE.

I—I don't—think of that.

THEOPHILA.

Well, I can't say anything more than—I'm
sorry.

> [OLIVE *rises, and, with faltering steps, comes
> to her.*

Olive.

Excuse me being so persistent. [*Piteously.*] You won't accept my help? [Theophila, *leaning back with closed eyes, shakes her head.*] You won't even—try?

Theophila.

[*Faintly, almost inaudibly.*] It would be of no use ; I couldn't.

Olive.

[*Drawing a long breath, her arms falling by her side.*] Ah !

Theophila.

I'm tired. Tell my sister——

Olive.

[*Goes to the upper door, opens it, and looks out.*] Oh, Quaife, where is Miss Emptage ?

Quaife.

[*Out of sight.*] In the dining-room, ma'am. Shall I——?

Olive.

[*Closing the door.*] No, thank you. [*She goes to the dining-room door, and opens it slightly, without withdrawing the portière.*] Miss Emptage !

Justina.

[*From the dining-room.*] Here !

OLIVE.

Your sister wishes to return to her room.

[OLIVE *walks away and stands outside the window as* JUSTINA *enters and goes to* THEOPHILA.

JUSTINA.

[*Raising* THEOPHILA.] Where's aunt? Why have they left you alone?

THEOPHILA.

I asked them to.

JUSTINA.

[*Lowering her voice.*] With *her?*

THEOPHILA.

Yes.

JUSTINA.

Tell me——!

THEOPHILA.

By and by. Take me away. [OLIVE *disappears.*

JUSTINA.

[*Walking with* THEOPHILA *towards the upper door.*] Oh, we've had such a time in there! Uncle Fletcher's been boring our heads off on the subject of the blessings of Arbitration ; and at last, Jack, who is in a vile temper, almost jumped down his throat.

> [*They go out, whereupon* JOHN *is seen to slightly push aside the portière and peep into the room. Satisfied that the room is empty, he enters quickly, closes the door behind him emphatically, and throws himself on to the settee with a groan of weariness.* OLIVE *returns ; she is about to pass the window, but seeing* JOHN, *she enters quietly, takes a chair, and sits. They remain looking at each other for a little while without speaking.*

OLIVE.

Good morning, John—well, afternoon.

JOHN.

Er—Have you lunched?

OLIVE.

No.

JOHN.

[*Looking towards the dining-room door.*]   It's in there.

OLIVE.

[*Dryly.*]   Thanks.

JOHN.

I—I'm sorry I can't offer to wait on you——

OLIVE.

Oh, pray don't——!

JOHN.

But Portwood is still eating.   I've been rude to him.

OLIVE.

Indeed ?

JOHN.

[*Rising and walking about.*] I believe all these people will drive me crazy !   I don't know where to get to for them.

OLIVE.

You are in your own house.   Need you seek to avoid any of them ?

JOHN.

Well, I'm not particularly desirous, for instance, of another encounter with Mr. Fraser.

OLIVE.

Another.   Have you—— ?

JOHN.

Yes.   I've been rude to him.

OLIVE.

Oh ! Mrs. Cloys——?

JOHN.

She treats me as a schoolmistress would treat a very small boy in disgrace.

OLIVE.

Miss Emptage——!

JOHN.

Lectures me and patronises me till my blood
curdles.   Just now I was almost—well, I hope
not——

OLIVE.

Rude to her?

JOHN.

Yes.   And then this maddening old man——?
I can't endure it!   Even my servants——

OLIVE.

Servants?

JOHN.

A minute or two ago I was trying to escape
from the dining-room by passing through the
kitchen, and I came upon my cook and Mrs.
Fraser's maid discussing me over a bowl of
chicken broth.   Mrs. Quaife—my cook——!   I
heard her distinctly!   "I never thought Mr.
Allingham was that sort of a gentleman," she
said.

OLIVE.

What sort of a gentleman?

JOHN.

I don't know.   I got away.

OLIVE.

H'm, I think I should have been rude to *her.*

JOHN.

And there are two more relatives of Mrs.
Fraser's to arrive yet.   [*Throwing himself into*

a chair.]   The boy has gone to town to fetch the mother.   The mother !

OLIVE.

[*Rising and walking towards the door.*]   At any rate, I can rid you of one unwelcome guest. [*He looks up at her.*]   I am going, John, directly.

JOHN.

Going home ?

OLIVE.

Going back to my flat.

JOHN.

[*Rising.*]   Then there is no longer any necessity for me to stick in this wretched cottage.

OLIVE.

I'm sorry to have been the cause——

JOHN.

Of course, I could not leave you here among your—your——

OLIVE.

Enemies.

JOHN.

Well, hardly friends.   Then Mrs. Fraser is well enough to travel ?

OLIVE.

I don't know, I'm sure.

JOHN.

You've relinquished your intention of devoting yourself to her?

OLIVE.

No, I haven't relinquished it.   Mrs. Fraser will have nothing to do with me.

JOHN.

She has said so?

OLIVE.

[*Sitting upon the settee.*]   Oh, yes, she has said so.

JOHN.

What reason does she give?

OLIVE.

She will not receive help from the woman who —who brought that humiliation on her last night. I believe, if she was starving, she wouldn't take a crust from my hand.

JOHN.

She returns to her husband, I suppose? .

OLIVE.

I think not.   She is in the mood to accept nothing from anybody.

JOHN.

[*Sitting with his head bowed.*]   Wounded— wounded——

OLIVE.

[*With a slight shrug of the shoulders.*] She's a sentimental, romantic little person, I find. Well——!

JOHN.

Ha, we didn't calculate for this when we arranged our ingenious little plan last night ! We were to restore Mrs. Fraser's name and position to her untarnished ; we were to set poor little Humpty-Dumpty up again by—when was it ?— Goodwood week; all in return for your ten minutes' fun in there ! We were d——d generous, you and I—only we reckoned without Mrs. Fraser ! [*Starting up.*] And so, you see, after all, we've had our fun and enjoyed it, and yet pay nothing for it ! But, at the same time, we mustn't forget that in this world everything has to be paid for by somebody. By Jove, there's no doubt as to who stands treat for last night ! Mrs. Fraser pays ! that poor, little, broken-down woman pays ! *She* pays——!

OLIVE.

[*Rising.*] You blame me beyond all reason ! I'll not put up with it ! Why didn't you call her aunt into the room last night when you saw Mrs. Fraser becoming wilder and wilder ? [*Walking away.*] Pah ! you appeared moonstruck ! moonstruck !

JOHN.

I thought I might save her from meeting her people while she was so unlike herself. You know I was helpless—— [*She approaches ; he seizes*

her by the shoulders.] You—you reproach me!
Why didn't you strike that bell sooner? why
didn't you strike it sooner? [*Leaving her, and
throwing himself into a chair.*] Ah, you weren't
capable even of that!

OLIVE.

[*Tearfully, rubbing her shoulders.*] Oh,
John——!

JOHN.

I beg your pardon.

OLIVE.

[*Going to him slowly, leaning against the
balustrade.*] John——

JOHN.

Well?

OLIVE.

I will confess it to you—I didn't strike the bell
at all.

JOHN.

You—did not?

OLIVE.

I was under the impression I had stopped the
clock before I sat down to listen, but in my agitation I must have shaken it and started it again.
[*Kneeling beside* JOHN's *chair.*] The clock struck
of its own accord.

JOHN.

And you sat there, drinking in every word; and
when the poor creature had cleared herself, and

satisfied you, still you made no effort——!
[*Rising.*] Oh !

OLIVE.

[*Seizing his coat.*] John, I *couldn't* move from
that curtain ! I was a wretch ! Pity me ! I
couldn't stir ! [JOHN *walks away. She rises from
the ground and sits.*] Oh, get me a carriage of
some sort to take me to the station.

JOHN.

[*Going towards the bell.*] I'll tell Quaife.
[*Pausing, looking at her.*] I don't know—I can't
imagine—how you are going to get through your
life——

OLIVE.

Oh, please ! I've been lectured by Mrs. Fraser,
Oh, there are heaps of solitary women in the
world ; some people envy them. [*He sits upon
the settee.*] Now that—now that—the chances
of our coming together again have fallen through,
I shall be off out of London at once. Where can
one go to at this time of the year ?

JOHN.

[*Abstractedly.*] Eh ? Er—it's a bit early for
most places.

OLIVE.

I'm going to Aix in August.

JOHN.

[*Looking up.*] You are ?

OLIVE.

Oh ! Why, did *you* think of——?

JOHN.

Yes. But it doesn't matter.

OLIVE.

Oh, I don't want to interfere with your——

JOHN.

Aix is a pretty big place.

OLIVE.

Where will you stay ?

JOHN.

I've been told, the " Splendide "——

OLIVE.

Oh——!

JOHN.

What ?

OLIVE.

I can easily put up elsewhere.

JOHN.

You needn't. I daresay the " Splendide " is quite large enough for two people who—who——

OLIVE.

Who want to keep far apart. [*Rising and going towards the door, pausing by the head of the settee.*] How ridiculous that reconciliation of ours last night? Why, how many weeks should we have been together?

JOHN.

[*His head resting upon his hands.*] Not many—not many, I'm afraid.

OLIVE.

Weeks! Days, I should have said—or hours. "Heaven have mercy upon us! we're reconciled!" Do you remember—last night——?

JOHN.

Ha! yes.

OLIVE.

"Heaven have mercy upon us!" Ha, ha!

JOHN.

Heaven have mercy on us!

OLIVE.

[*Wiping the tears from her eyes.*] I—I'll go and put my bonnet on. [*He rises, and she holds out her hand.*] Good-bye, John.

JOHN.

[*Taking her hand, looking away.*] Good-bye.

OLIVE.

[*Suddenly drawing back.*] Oh——!

JOHN.

What?

OLIVE.

[*Breathlessly.*]   Oh, yes——!

JOHN.

Olive ?

OLIVE.

Ah—h—h—h, you'll find plenty of pretty women at Aix——!

QUAIFE *enters, showing in* MRS. EMTAGE *and* CLAUDE. QUAIFE *retires.* MRS. EMPTAGE *is in a bright and fashionable morning dress.*

MRS. EMPTAGE.

[*To* OLIVE.]   Mrs. Allingham——!   [*To* CLAUDE.]   Claude, keep by me. My legs are all of a tremble. Where is my daughter, Mrs. Fraser ? Take me to her. I am very ill indeed ; I fancy this affair has affected my heart——

JOHN.

Pray sit down for a moment.

MRS. EMPTAGE.

[*Sitting down.*]   We used to be friends, Mr. Allingham—great friends ; now I wonder you can look me in the face. [*Panting.*]   I have heard everything from Claude. I am ashamed—I must say it—I am ashamed of you and your wife.

[OLIVE *makes a movement as if to go ;* JOHN *detains her.*

JOHN.

[*To* OLIVE.] No, no ; I don't think we'll run away and hide any more. [*Turning to* MRS. EMPTAGE.] But I hope that Mrs. Emptage will be kind enough to apply to me, alone, any harsh expressions she may care to make use of——

SIR FLETCHER *enters.*

SIR FLETCHER PORTWOOD.

[*Advancing.*] Ah, Muriel——!

MRS. EMPTAGE.

[*Rising, throwing her arms round* SIR FLETCHER'S *neck.*] Oh, Fletcher, Fletcher ! I've hardly closed my eyes all night !

CLAUDE.

May I ask what has gone on during my absence ?

SIR FLETCHER PORTWOOD.

During *your* absence—— !

MRS. EMPTAGE.

Is Alec here ?

SIR FLETCHER PORTWOOD.

Yes, the family gathering is complete.

MRS. EMPTAGE.

Does Theo return to Lennox Gardens ? Has an arrangement of any sort been come to ?

Sir Fletcher Portwood.

None that I know of.   I seem to be powerless.

Mrs. Cloys and Fraser enter.

Claude.

[*Meeting them.*]   'Ullo, aunt! 'ullo, Fraser!
 [Mrs. Emptage, *totters to* Mrs. Cloys.
  Claude *retires.* John *walks away to*
  the fireplace. Olive *is now seated*
  upon the settee.

Mrs. Emptage.

[*Embracing* Mrs. Cloys.] Oh, Harriet, I am
very poorly; I don't think I have had two hours'
rest all night. [*Going to* Fraser *and kissing
him.*]   Alec you will prove a generous, good fellow—of that I am sure.   Poor Theo has behaved
very indiscreetly.   I really believe my heart has
been upset by it all——

Mrs. Cloys.

I have something important to say, Muriel.
Pray sit down and be quiet.

Mrs. Emptage.

[*In a flutter.*]   I know, I know.   Unless I can
be kept quiet it will be very serious for me.   [*In
her agitation she is about to sit upon the settee
beside* Olive.]   Oh, dear, what am I doing!
[*Moving away, she stops, pointing to the library.*]
Great Heavens! was that the room——?

Mrs. Cloys.

S-s-sh ! [Mrs. Emptage *sits again.* Fraser *goes to the window and stands there, apart, his back turned to those in the room.*] What I have to say concerns the future of Theophila—— [*There is a movement on the part of* John *and* Olive.] Please let nobody go. All who are here are interested in the future of Mrs. Fraser— [*looking at* Olive]—and I believe sympathetically interested. [*Sitting.*] In fact, I want it to be known that a very happy arrangement has been arrived at.

Mrs. Emptage.

[*To* Sir Fletcher.] Fletcher, you said *no* arrangement had been arrived at.

Sir Fletcher.

I have not been consulted, Harriet.

Mrs. Cloys.

I did not consider it necessary, Fletcher. There was a question whether the plan I had in view *could* be carried out.

Sir Fletcher.

Then you—you have constituted yourself a— a sort of—arbitrator——

Mrs. Cloys.

As you say, a sort of arbitratrix, I suppose.

SIR FLETCHER PORTWOOD.

The cloak of pedantry, Harriet, scarcely con-
ceals your want of respect for your brother.

[*Passing* MRS. CLOYS, *as if about to quit
the room.*

MRS. CLOYS.

[*Touching his arm.*] We'll all keep our tempers,
Fletcher. [*He remains.*]   Yes, the thought came
to me during the night—a long, anxious night——

MRS. EMPTAGE.

Ah, indeed !

MRS. CLOYS.

The thought that I would telegraph to the
bishop the very first thing this morning.

SIR FLETCHER PORTWOOD.

The bishop !

MRS. CLOYS.

Asking him to come to me at once.

SIR FLETCHER PORTWOOD.

Will he do so ?

MRS. CLOYS.

The bishop is goodness and compliance per-
sonified.   He left St. Olpherts at ten o'clock this
morning ; he is here.

SIR FLETCHER PORTWOOD.

Here !

Mrs. Emptage.

I shall be ashamed to meet him; after my sleepless night my face is so dreadfully lined——!

Mrs. Cloys.

The bishop does not notice the lines in women's faces. Directly he arrived, I submitted my scheme; in two words, he approved; it will be carried into execution.

Sir Fletcher Portwood.

I do not ask *what* scheme.

Mrs. Cloys.

Theophila returns to St. Olpherts at once with us. She will rest there two or three days, by which time I shall have found a suitable house in town——

Mrs. Emptage.

In town——?

Mrs. Cloys.

The bishop and I have not had a house in town for some years. Mr. Fraser kindly sees house agents this afternoon.

Sir Fletcher Portwood.

I would willingly have seen house agents, Harriet. A furnished house——?

Mrs. Cloys.

[*Assenting.*] For the season—sufficiently large for the dear bishop, myself, and Theophila. Both

in London and at St. Olpherts, Theophila will be
my close companion.   In our little London gaieties
she will figure prominently.   At certain formal
gatherings she will share the responsibilities of the
hostess.   If any paragraph concerning our doings
should creep into the newspaper, it will concern
the Bishop of St. Olpherts, Mrs. Cloys, *and* Mrs.
Fraser of Locheen.   Oh, I don't think there will
be many to wag evil tongues against Mrs. Fraser
a few months hence !

> [OLIVE *rises and advances to* MRS. CLOYS,
> *who stands up as she approaches.*

OLIVE.

[*In a low voice, to* MRS. CLOYS.]   I'm glad ; I'm
very glad.

MRS. CLOYS.

That's right.

OLIVE.

[*Falteringly.*]   But your—your scheme owes—
just a little to my idea, doesn't it ?

MRS. CLOYS.

I admit it.   Mrs. Allingham, I am sure you don't
grudge——

OLIVE.

No, no ; indeed I don't.   I—I hope you will
succeed—to the utmost——

> [*She turns away, and goes out by the dining-
> room door.*

MRS. EMPTAGE.

[*Rising, fretfully.*] It seems to me everything is taken out of one's hands——

SIR FLETCHER.

In a most unceremonious way——

MRS. EMPTAGE.

[*Glancing at* FRASER, *who is now out in the garden.*] What about Alec—Mr. Fraser——?

SIR FLETCHER.

Of course, any policy that doesn't tend to bring my niece and her husband together——

MRS. CLOYS.

Ah, I haven't told you. Mr. Fraser is to be a frequent—a fairly frequent visitor in London, and at St. Olpherts.

SIR FLETCHER.

[*With a sniff.*] Visitor——

MRS. CLOYS.

And it is further arranged that, in a year's time, Mr. Fraser comes to us and formally asks Theophila to return to Lennox Gardens.

MRS. EMPTAGE.

And when he does——?

MRS. CLOYS.

Then we shall see what we shall see.

SIR FLETCHER.

[*Walking away.*] I can't quite explain my feeling—but I am not sanguine—not at all sanguine.

MRS. EMPTAGE.

At any rate, in less than twelve months, if I know my girl, she will have grown heartily sick of her solemn surroundings.

MRS. CLOYS.

[*Indignantly.*] How dare you——! How——! [*Checking herself.*] Well, suppose she *does* weary of me, good will result even from *that* if it sends her back to her husband.

The door opens, and the BISHOP OF ST. OLPHERTS *enters with* THEOPHILA *upon his arm.* JUSTINA *follows them, carrying a shawl. The bishop is a mild looking, very old man.* THEOPHILA *is dressed in her cape and bonnet, and her face is hidden under her thick veil.*

THEOPHILA.

[*Coming to* MRS. EMPTAGE, *and kissing her.*] Mother——

[MRS. EMPTAGE *kisses her hastily and bustles over to the* BISHOP.

MRS. EMPTAGE.

Ah, bishop, I can hardly hope you'll recollect me.

BISHOP.

[*Vaguely.*] Yes, yes, yes.

Mrs. Emptage.
[*With a simper.*] Muriel, you know.

Bishop.
[*Taking her hand.*] Mrs. Emptage—— !

Mrs. Emptage.
Don't tell me ; I know I'm altered.

Bishop.
Ah, years pass over us.

Mrs. Emptage.
It isn't that—but I had no sleep last night.
    [Sir Fletcher *advances, and grasps the*
      Bishop's *hand.*

Sir Fletcher.
I remember years ago, at the opening of the
People's Library at Stockwell, describing Dr.
Cloys as one of the stoutest pillars of our
Church——

Bishop.
[*Uneasily.*] The People's Library at——?

Sir Fletcher.
Stockwell. To-day I have only to add—may
that pillar never grow faint nor weary ; may its
back remain equal to the burden imposed upon it ;

may it continue to plough the stormy seas of
scepticism and agnosticism !

BISHOP.

[*Helplessly.*]   Er-r—who is it ?

MRS. CLOYS.

My brother Fletcher.

BISHOP.

Ah, how do you do ?   [QUAIFE *appears.*

MRS. CLOYS.

Is the fly here ?

QUAIFE.

Yes, ma'am.
      [QUAIFE *withdraws.   The* BISHOP *moves
      towards the window,* SIR FLETCHER
      closely following him.

THEOPHILA.

[*To* MRS. EMPTAGE.]   Good-bye, mother dear.

MRS. EMPTAGE.

[*Embracing her.*]   Oh, good-bye, my darling. I
won't reproach you.   If you make a bed you must
lie on it.   You've nearly broken my heart, but
I'm only your mother——

THEOPHILA.

Oh, don't—— !

Mrs. Emptage.

[*In a whisper.*] Mind you see that we visit you constantly in London and St. Olpherts !

Theophila.

Yes, yes. [*As she is walking away, she sees* John—*who has been standing silently behind the settee, his back turned to those in the room—and she says to the others.*] One moment. [*She comes down, looking at* John.] Mr. Allingham. [*He approaches her slowly. After a pause, she says in a low voice.*] Oh, Jack, how could you? [*He bows his head, making no reply.*] Well—for auld lang-syne—— [*She holds out her hand; he takes it, but releases it quickly. She turns to go, then pauses.*] Where's your wife? [*He looks towards the dining-room door. She hesitates for a moment, then goes out quickly by that door.*]

Mrs. Cloys.

[*Looking round.*] Theophila—Theophila——

John.

[*Watching the door.*] She will be here in a moment, she is with my wife.

Sir Fletcher Portwood.

[*His voice rising.*] My dear bishop, it is my view of life, and the observation has some theological bearing, that the devil almost invariably appears to women in the form of Impulse. In saying this, I am perhaps on the verge of a truism——

BISHOP OF ST. OLPHERTS.
No, no, no.

THEOPHILA *re-enters ; her veil is raised.*

THEOPHILA.
[*As she passes* JOHN, *lowering her veil.*] It's all right.

> [*There is a hubbub of talk as* THEOPHILA *and her relatives go out at the upper door.*

MRS. EMPTAGE.
You will need a warm wrap, Theo.

JUSTINA.
I have one here, mother.

MRS. CLOYS.
Now, bishop——

SIR FLETCHER PORTWOOD.
Is the carriage closed?

BISHOP OF ST. OLPHERTS.
I hope not.

SIR FLETCHER PORTWOOD.
You shall run no risk, my dear bishop——

Mrs. Emptage.

Claude, come to the gate. Give me your arm,
Alec——

> [*The talk ceases.* John *is alone. After a
> pause he goes out into the garden and
> stands looking off towards the left, as
> if watching the departing carriage.*
> Olive *enters slowly and sadly ; she sits
> upon the settee, covering her eyes with
> her hand.* John *re-enters the room.
> Seeing* Olive, *he remains where he is
> for a moment or two irresolutely ; then
> he comes down to her, sits beside her,
> and takes her hand.*

THE END.

www.ingramcontent.com/pod-product-compliance
Lightning Source LLC
Chambersburg PA
CBHW030102030726
47498CB00007B/2226